# Lakeside University Cover Up

## by Charles A. Taylor

ISBN #0-935483-53-5

# DEDICATION

This book is dedicated to college students everywhere who are committed to a just and compassionate society that celebrates diversity while working for the common good.

# CONTENTS

# ACKNOWLEDGEMENTS

I have many people to thank for the completion of this novel, first and foremost, my wife Camilla, for reading numerous drafts and for her constant words of encouragement. I'd also like to thank my first editor Nancy Richardson for helping me start this writing odyssey nearly nine years ago. Last year I made up my mind to finish the novel and although it took nearly a decade, it's finally done. I was fortunate to find my current editor Carrie Kilman who helped me to make this a better work.

I must also send a 'shout-out' to my long-term friend Elizabeth Johanna for formatting the manuscript.

Many friends and kin folk read copies of the manuscript and your suggestions, no doubt has made this a better reading. You have my sincerest gratitude. Finally, a special thanks to the wonderful students and staff I've met over the years when facilitating retreats at different college campuses. Many of the characters in this book were inspired by your search for truth and justice.

## CHAPTER ONE

Enough was enough. Dean of Students, Todd Severson stormed into President David Horning's office and slammed the door. "Sir, we need to do something!" Severson said, lowering himself into the chair across from Horning's antique desk. "Your divide and conquer strategy is backfiring—we have to do something and do it fast, or this university will explode!"

President Horning glanced up from his coffee. "That's a bit dramatic, Todd, don't you think?"

Severson leaned forward in his chair and pressed his palms against the desktop. "A black student has just been attacked!" he said. "Classes are being disrupted. The police are running themselves ragged, trying to keep everything under control. Now we have threats of a major civil rights demonstration being held on our campus!"

Horning looked at Severson and frowned. "Why don't you just calm down," he said. "We've weathered crises before. This isn't any different."

Severson stared back, his jaw askew. "Sir, I beg to disagree! We may have been able to smooth things over in the past, but this is very different. This could turn violent—even more violent than it already has become. And it's just a matter of time before the media plasters this mess all over the front page."

Before Horning could respond, his phone rang. As he reached to answer it, Severson stood to leave. "Hold on Todd. Let me get this. This might be the call that will get us out of this damn mess," Horning said, as Severson paced the floor.

\*\*\*

1

# Three Weeks Earlier

It was a cool, cloudy Sunday night in early autumn. Two figures huddled in the shadows next to a small house, near the Lakeside University campus. They set to work quickly, and soon a sharp chemical odor drifted through the air.

"Man, this shit really stinks," said the first one, muffling a cough in his gloved hand. "Are you sure this will work?"

"It has to," said the second. "You heard what they said. We've got to take care of this tonight."

"Okay, okay," said the first. "Just light the damn thing so I can make the call and we can get the hell out of here!"

\*\*\*

Inside the small house, Lakeside University student Ashante Melashe was working on a recording for her broadcast engineering class. Just as she hit the *record* button, the shrill ring of the telephone echoed through the house. "Oh, no!" she moaned, "I forgot to turn off the ringer!" She pushed her chair back from the table. "Well, that's another sound bite down the drain."

"I'm coming," she grumbled as the phone continued its loud summons. "Hello?"

"Look outside," said a gruff, male voice. "You'll see how we feel about *niggers* at Lakeside University."

"What did you just say? Who is this?"

"Just look outside, bitch"

"Is this some kind of joke?" Ashante asked, but the only answer was the dial tone.

Shaking her head in disgust, she took a deep breath and stepped out into the front yard. The shock of the flames sucked the air from her lungs in a choked gasp. A strange smell burned her eyes and throat. She stood frozen, glaring at the blaze of bright red and orange fire burning against the cold, black starless night.

Then the realization hit her with as much force as if someone had kicked her in the stomach. Suddenly she knew what she was staring at: a huge cross, whose wicked flames lit up the yard and filled her with soul wrenching horror.

"Oh, my God," Ashante whispered.

\*\*\*

Five miles away, Gloria Wilson stifled a yawn and tried to find a more comfortable position behind the wheel of her Corolla. The dashboard clock read 10:31 p.m.

"Almost there," she said aloud. "It's a good thing," she added with a laugh, "since I've been talking to myself for the last half hour. I swear this drive gets longer every time."

She leaned forward to change the CD, and hummed along with *Usher*. The first sign announcing the Lakeside University exit loomed out of the darkness along the highway. She breathed a sigh of relief; she still had homework to finish for tomorrow, and she really didn't want to be up all night.

As much as Gloria dreaded this three-hour drive, it was worth it for a weekend with her family. A weekend at home brought flavors of cornbread and greens, slow jams, old-time religious services, and talk that didn't need explaining.

Her family's pride in her achievements always gave Gloria a boost in confidence. They didn't always express their pride in words, but it showed in other ways. Her momma insisted on doing Gloria's laundry, fussed about whether she was getting enough to eat at college, and worried about the "bland cafeteria food."

Momma always had some words of advice, whether Gloria wanted to hear them or not. Her daddy would slip her twenty dollars and a wink as he told her goodbye. Her younger brother,

Anthony, had steadily improved his grades in high school ever since Gloria had enrolled at Lakeside.

Her mind wandered to thoughts of how she had ended up at Lakeside. Mr. Ed Brown, Lakeside's lone black recruiter, visited her high school on a recruiting trip. Gloria met with him out of curiosity but was quickly impressed by his easy manner and willingness to answer her questions. He seemed to listen carefully to her jigsaw puzzle of concerns.

She told him that her dream was to become a college professor and that she had been told that a large research university was the best place to attend. He calmly discussed the advantages that a small school like Lakeside offered. He told her about Lakeside's reputation for producing great teachers and how each student was carefully mentored during the senior year. For the first time Gloria found herself seriously considering Lakeside and after she toured the campus, she made the decision to enroll.

Spending the weekend at home with family, reminded Gloria how alone she sometimes felt at Lakeside—where she was one of only 70 blacks, on a campus of more than 4,000 students. When she decided to enroll at Lakeside, she thought being at a small school in a small town might force her to focus on her studies. She could hear her momma's words; "booking" was what she was there for anyway. Her momma said if she was strong enough to leave home, she was strong enough to face the world head on. Gloria wasn't as sure as her momma but she took comfort in knowing that with three of her friends attending, she would have a small but strong support network.

But two of her friends transferred to other schools by the end of their freshman year. They thought Lakeside was 'too rural and too conservative'. If it hadn't been for Ashante, Gloria knew she probably would have left Lakeside, too. She smiled when she thought of her roommate—so flashy and bold, where Gloria was bookish and uncertain. Where Ashante flirted, Gloria hid behind

4

her wire-frame glasses and loose-fitting clothes. Gloria's parents certainly didn't mind that their naturally beautiful daughter seemed to find no interest in dating just yet, but Gloria knew Ashante loved to tease her for it.

Gloria signaled and took the first Westport exit ramp. She leaned forward in an unconscious effort to speed the car along. "Well, I finally made it back," she said softly. As she rounded the first corner into the neighborhood, she heard boxes shift in the backseat. The boxes were filled with African crafts, kinte cloth and beads. *Ashante is gonna be surprised when she sees all the cool stuff I've brought back for the house*, she thought.

She and Ashante had just moved into the house a few weeks earlier, at the start of their junior year. In a town where rentals were hard to come by, they saw the ad and couldn't believe their luck. That had been sight unseen however. When they'd stepped foot inside the place, they weren't sure "luck" was the right word. The floors were strewn with empty beer cans and pizza boxes; the stove was caked with years' worth of dried food; the matted carpeting smelled like stale beer.

All the landlord said about the previous tenants was that he'd evicted them. And the only question he really seemed to ask Gloria and Ashante was whether they were drug users. Ashante had bristled at that—"Is he asking because we're black?" she'd whispered to Gloria through gritted teeth. They had been ready to give up on "the dump" as Ashante had called it, when the landlord promised that his cleaning crew would be in to fix it up. He also promised to replace the carpeting in all the rooms and to paint the interior of the house. The place had its redeeming qualities—a bedroom for each of them and plenty of storage space in the attic. Besides most rentals had already been taken for the fall. They crossed their fingers and signed the lease that day.

Gloria rounded the final corner. *Almost there*, she thought. And then she saw the flames. For an instant, she thought the house was on fire and nearly lost control of the car. Then reality hit her like a slap across the face—a cross burning in their yard lighting up the night, as if the sky itself were on fire.

Gloria gasped. She slowed her car to a stop, barely noticing the neighbors and students who had gathered in their yard. The sight filled Gloria with a sudden dread—the kind of dread she didn't yet have words for. Suddenly, she saw Ashante emerge from the crowd, her face streaked with tears.

Ashante ran up to the car. "G.W., G.W., look what they've done! Just look!" Ashante yelled through the window.

But Gloria couldn't take her eyes off the flames. She parked her car at the curb and stumbled out. The air was filled with a thick, choking smoke. The heat from the blaze stung her cheeks as if she had been smacked.

She looked at Ashante. "Why us?" Gloria asked in a hoarse whisper. "Why?"

Ashante just shook her head because she had no answer.

Gloria pushed her way around the crowd and moved toward the driveway, oblivious to the murmured condolences and words of outrage and disbelief from the neighbors and students who had gathered there. She was too shocked to notice the sympathetic hands that reached for her, knowing only that she felt terribly, horribly sick.

A newspaper reporter pushed a tape recorder in front of Gloria's face. "Is this your home?" he said. "Any idea who could have done this?"

Gloria shoved past him. The smoke burned her nose and throat, and a bitter taste filled her mouth. She sank to her knees on the driveway and vomited, as the reporter's flashbulb flashed again and again nearby. All around her, people were talking, their faces illuminated by the light of the flames.

"Who would do such a thing?" a young woman kept asking. "Who?"

"How awful for G.W. and Ashante."

"Shouldn't someone call the fire department?"

"I told you they don't like blacks here!"

"Where are the police?"

No one seemed to have any answers.

*The police*, Gloria thought, *I need to call the campus police*. She started toward the house, but Chuck Johnson, a black football star at Lakeside, blocked her path. Chuck was clutching the front of Chris Polaski's shirt. Chris was a thin, redheaded, white student whom Gloria recognized from her sociology class.

"Cool it, Chuck, will you?" Chris was pleading, as he struggled to free himself from Chuck's grip. "All I said was, 'It was probably just a frat prank, nothing serious.' I didn't mean anything by that."

"It may not seem serious to you," Chuck said, "but then you never have to worry about anyone calling you names or burning a cross in your yard, do you, cracker?"

Gloria cleared her throat. "What's going on?" she said.

Chuck glared at him, before releasing his hold on Chris's shirt. Chris gave Gloria a quick, grateful nod and disappeared into the crowd, leaving Gloria and Chuck standing at the edge of the driveway.

Chuck turned to Gloria and gave her a hug. "Hey sister, I'm really sorry," he said, as Gloria felt tears well up in her eyes. "Don't worry," Chuck said. "They'll catch the bastards who did this."

Gloria nodded, though she felt anything but reassured. Instead, she scanned the crowd for Ashante. Where had she gone?

"Chuck," she said, "I need to find Ashante. We need to call the police!"

"I think someone already—," Chuck started to say, but a commotion erupted on the far side of the crowd, as they both turned to look.

A tall, handsome, young man was shouldering his way across the yard, gripping a large, red fire extinguisher. The crowd parted to let him through and as he approached the burning cross, his dark skin glistened with sweat in the light from the flames. Even from a slight distance, Gloria could see the fury on his face.

He triggered the extinguisher and a spray of white foam hit the flames with a *hiss*. The crowd fell silent. Gloria watched as the flames turned orange and black around the edges; at first the fire seemed to fight back—it curled away from the foam, dancing out of reach. *Like the flames of Hell*, Gloria thought to herself.

But the man kept spraying and soon most of the flames died in a hiss of steam and smoke under the foamy onslaught. As the fire was being snuffed out, Gloria could see swaths of charred wood, dark as tar, some of the pieces already crumbling and falling away. Finally, only the very top of the cross still burned, a single flame licking at the cold, black sky.

All around her, the crowd seemed to hold its breath. And Gloria, despite the desperation she had felt to get away from all of this, suddenly felt glued to the spot. She waited and watched as the young man paused, then he raised his extinguisher and sprayed until the last flame went out.

Ashante walked over and stood at Gloria's side. Together, they watched as the young man pushed his way out through the crowd without a word, toward the street.

Gloria turned to Ashante. "Who was that?" she asked.

"Jamal Washington," Ashante said.

Chuck Johnson, who was still standing on the driveway, leaned in. "They call him Little Malcolm because Malcolm X is his hero, " Chuck said." He's head of the BSO—the Black Student Organization on campus."

"Is he a friend of yours?" Gloria asked.

"He's not really the social type," Chuck said. "Jamal's a race man. That brother ain't got time for nobody unless they're part of the cause, if you know what I'm sayin'."

Suddenly, Gloria heard heavy footsteps coming up behind her. "Is this your house?" a gruff voice asked, and a hand encircled Gloria's arm in a strong grip.

## CHAPTER TWO

Gloria turned and found herself face-to-face with two police officers, one heavy-set, the other tall and thin.

"I asked, 'Do you live here'?" said the heavy-set cop.

Gloria nodded.

"Do you live alone?"

"No, she's my roommate," Gloria said, nodding toward Ashante.

"I'm Sergeant George Thomas, and this is Sergeant Ralph Carlson. We need to ask you some questions. Can we go inside, away from this crowd?"

Gloria nodded and led the way, with a silent Ashante trailing behind. They walked past the smoldering remains of the cross. The house door was wide open as they stepped inside. With one last look at the crowd, Gloria shut the door behind them.

"Now then, I'll need both of your names for the record," Sgt. Thomas said.

Gloria and Ashante glanced at each other.

"Gloria Wilson," Gloria said.

"Ashante Melashe," Ashante said.

Sgt. Thomas looked up from his notebook. "What is that, African or something?" he said. "How do you spell that?"

Ashante bit her lip, and then recited the letters, one by one.

"Okay, and how long have you lived here?" Sgt. Thomas asked them.

Gloria answered. "Just since the start of the semester," she said. "Less than a month."

"Were you both here at the time of the incident?" Sgt. Carlson asked.

Ashante shook her head. "I was here alone," she said. "G.W.—I mean, Gloria—wasn't back yet."

Sgt. Carlson turned to Gloria. "Where were you?" he said.

"On my way back from visiting my parents for the weekend."

Sgt. Carlson glanced at something in his notes, and then trained his eyes on Ashante.

"When did you first become aware of the incident?" he asked her.

"I got a phone call telling me to go look outside."

"Do you know who called?" Sgt. Thomas asked.

Ashante shook her head. "He had the caller I.D. blocked. And I didn't recognize his voice."

"What exactly did the caller say?" Sgt. Carlson asked.

Ashante hesitated, and her eyes filled with tears. Gloria moved closer to her friend and gently squeezed her arm.

"He said, 'Hey bitch, look outside and see how we feel about *niggers* at our college'." Ashante's voice was barely more than a whisper. "Then he hung up."

Gloria sucked in a sharp breath. "He said that?" she said.

But before Ashante could answer, Sgt. Carlson sighed impatiently. "When you got outside, the cross was already burning?" he asked.

Ashante nodded.

"Did you see anyone suspicious?"

"No," Ashante said. "People were already starting to come because of the flames. I'm sure whoever started it was long gone."

"How long were you outside?"

"Until you all got here—at least half an hour."

"That's about enough time," Sgt. Thomas said to Sgt. Carlson.

"Enough time for what?" Gloria asked.

Sgt. Thomas shook his head. "Nothing," he said. "We just need to know how much time passed between the call and the cross burning for the record. So has anything like this happened before?"

"No, like I said, we've only been renting this house for a few weeks," Gloria answered. She thought for a second, then glanced at her roommate. "But wait. A few days ago, Ashante caught a guy looking through our window. The campus police know about it. We reported it."

Gloria and Ashante looked at each other, a startled expression on both of their faces.

"Speaking of the campus police," Gloria said, "why aren't they handling this? I thought this was still their jurisdiction."

Sgt. Carlson cleared his throat. "Well, he said, 'you're right this isn't our normal jurisdiction. We're only helping out because they're a little short-handed tonight." He closed his notebook and glanced around the living room, at the shelves of African art and framed pictures of high school friends. "So," he said, "one more time. Do you know who did this?"

Gloria's eyes widened. "What? Of course we don't! Why aren't you talking to the students outside? Somebody may have seen something!"

"We'll get around to them," Sgt. Carlson said, "but for now this looks like just another campus prank."

For the first time since her arrival, anger replaced Gloria's fear.

"Prank!" Gloria said. "Are you serious? All that was missing was a rope and white robes. This was malicious! It was supposed to frighten us. My momma would say they knew they were doing evil and they did it anyway."

But when Sgt. Thomas spoke, his voice was hard and cold. "Are you sure you or your roommate haven't done anything to provoke this type of incident?"

Gloria felt the blood rushing to her face, and she willed herself to stay calm. "Other than being born black, you mean?" she said. "You've got to be kidding me. Nothing justifies what happened tonight."

"Have you made any enemies—you know what I mean," Sgt. Thomas said.

"No, I don't. And why do you keep saying 'incident', like using a clinical term can somehow make this less painful?" Gloria said, becoming increasingly upset. "They burned a cross in our yard! A cross! And they called us '*niggers*'!"

Sgt. Carlson took a step forward. "What my partner is trying to say is, we don't know who did it or why. No one should start jumping to conclusions. You're not going to help the situation by crying racism here and calling for a witch-hunt when you have no evidence. I'm sure this is far less serious. After all, this is not the Deep South in the '60s."

"Yeah, that's what I meant," Sgt. Thomas said, skirting an apology. Then, abruptly, he said, "Is it okay if I use your john?"

Gloria tried to contain her anger. "I guess so," she said, when what she really wanted to do was tell them to get the hell out of their place. "Down the hall on the right."

They watched Sgt. Thomas disappear around the corner, then Gloria turned to Sgt. Carlson. "Man, your line of questioning is really insulting," she said. "Racism didn't end in the '60s, you know, and it wasn't just confined to the Deep South."

"We're not trying to be unsympathetic," he said. "We just don't think it'll do any good to blow this out of proportion—."

Before he could finish, Sgt. Thomas returned from the bathroom. "We're done here," he told his partner, as he headed for the door. Sgt. Carlson followed him.

Gloria and Ashante followed them to the door. "You'll investigate this, right?" Ashante demanded.

Sgt. Carlson paused in the doorway. "There's not much to go on, but we'll look into it," he said, and then they left, walking past the dwindling crowd still assembled on the lawn.

Gloria and Ashante stared after them. Then Gloria exploded.

"We're the victims," she said, "and those mothers have the nerve to say we could have caused this? I can't believe it! We've got to report this to the campus police, Ashante, or to somebody who will actually do something."

"You know how cops are," Ashante said. "I suppose we shouldn't have expected anything else."

"I guess I never wanted to believe it until tonight. Those bastards treating us that way. I still don't know why they showed up instead of the campus cops."

A loud click startled them.

"What was that?" Gloria asked, looking around the room.

Ashante motioned toward her desk. "Don't worry—just my tape recorder. I was recording house noises for my sound-mixing class before all this mess started. I completely forgot about it!"

"You and your recordings," Gloria said, breaking the tension with a nervous laugh. "Last week you were recording yard noises; then shopping mall noises. What is it this week, insensitive-cop noises?"

Ashante laughed weakly, and Gloria noticed that Ashante's hands were shaking.

"Are you okay, girl?" Gloria said.

"I just realized, we may have the caller on tape—or at least my part of the conversation," Ashante said, in a quivering voice.

"Do you think you taped those redneck cops, too? Quick, let's rewind the tape!"

They both jumped as a loud knock sounded at the front door.

"Who is it?" Gloria demanded.

"Donna Sullivan," a voice called from outside.

Gloria pulled the curtain back and saw a young white woman standing on the front porch. "Ashante," Gloria said, "I'll take care of this. You get the tape ready."

Gloria opened the door and stepped out into the yard. The woman looked about Gloria's age, her hair in a ponytail, her expression earnest. "Did you say 'Donna'?" Gloria said, as she pulled the door shut.

"Yes, Donna Sullivan. Are you one of the students who live here?"

Gloria nodded. "Gloria Wilson," she said.

"Gloria, I just stopped by to say how sorry I am. As president of White Students Against Racism, I just want you to know how outraged we are over what happened. If there's anything we can do, I hope you'll tell us."

The interaction with the police fresh in her mind, Gloria was about to make a sarcastic retort. But she stopped when she realized the look of concern on this woman's face was real. Or at least, she corrected herself, it *seemed* real.

"Thanks," Gloria said. "I'll tell my roommate Ashante that."

There was an awkward moment of silence.

"Well, I'm sure you're exhausted, so I won't keep you," Donna said. She reached out, a small card in her hand. "Here's my address and number. Please, don't hesitate getting in touch with me."

"Thanks," Gloria said.

As Donna turned to go, Gloria looked out across the lawn and noticed most of the crowd had left. She wondered whether the police had questioned anyone. Somehow she doubted it. The few people who remained stood huddled in small groups, whispering and glancing at the charred wood still standing in the yard. She was relieved to see the reporter was gone.

On the far side of the yard, she saw Jamal engaged in a heated conversation with a group of students gathered in a small circle. He was talking with such force, she could hear him from across the lawn.

"Can't you see, this is just the beginning?" he was saying. "They think they can push us around and get away with it, and knowing the cops around here, they will. We need to do something. We need to make our voices heard. Otherwise, they might do something worse than burn a cross next time."

Gloria noticed the handful of listeners all nodded in approval, and she walked closer to hear better.

"They've struck the first blow," Jamal said. "Now it's our turn to show them we won't take this lying down."

With that, he stepped away from the group.

"Jamal?" Gloria said, approaching him.

"Can I help you?" he asked her.

"I just wanted to thank you for putting out the fire," she said. Noticing his blank look, she added, "I'm Gloria Wilson. I live here with Ashante."

"Oh," he said. "Well, I wouldn't take this too personally. This cross burning was aimed at all of us, not just you."

"Do you have any idea who might have done it?"

"If you're asking if I know their names, no. But they're the same type that burned homes and lynched our people in Alabama and Mississippi." As Jamal spoke, the intensity of his convictions lit up his eyes. "They hate us just because we're African people."

"Then you don't think it was just a prank?"

"Hell no, it wasn't a prank. It was a warning—a hate crime," Jamal said, and then he strode off into the darkness.

## CHAPTER THREE

G loria remembered Ashante's tape and walked quickly back to the house.

"Hey, I saw you talking with Jamal," Ashante said, as Gloria walked in. "What did he have to say?"

"I just wanted to thank him for putting out the fire," Gloria said. "He's not very easy to talk to."

"But he's easy to look at, girl," Ashante said with a smile. "Don't you think?"

Gloria rolled her eyes and ignored Ashante's question. Ashante had a boyfriend—they'd met at Lakeside, but now Tyrone was a law student in Pennsylvania. Ashante loved to flirt with guys, but she always made it clear that her heart belonged to no one but Tyrone.

Gloria normally didn't mind Ashante's jokes and nudges about how she should be more interested in dating—but right now she had other things on her mind.

"What about the tape," Gloria said. "Did you listen to it?"

Ashante shook her head. "I was waiting for you," she said.

Ashante had already rewound the tape. As she pressed *play*, they leaned forward expectantly, as the tape began to roll.

Even with the volume cranked as high as it would go, they could barely make out the sounds—the scrape of a chair on the floor, the *clink* of silverware on a plate, the steady drip of a faucet—all sounds Ashante commonly made while recording.

When they heard the ringing of the phone, Gloria leaned in closer. "This is it! Here!" she said.

They could hear the muffled sound of Ashante's voice in the background, but they couldn't hear any of the words. After the phone conversation, there was a short pause, and then they could hear other voices on the tape. They sounded like male voices, talking fast and angrily. But there was so much static and interference on the recording, it was impossible to make them out.

Gloria strained to listen. "I can't tell what they're saying," she said. "Those voices sound so far away. Were the windows open last night? Could that be the sound of all the people who were in our yard?"

Ashante frowned, thinking. "It must be," she finally said. "As soon as it happened, people started coming. Everyone was talking all at once, asking questions, trying to figure out what had happened. The recorder must've picked up the crowd noises."

"Still," Gloria said, "why do you think the tape is so fuzzy? Your recordings usually don't have static like this."

Ashante sat back in her chair and shook her head. "I don't know," she said, as the tape came to an end with a *pop*. "I'll take it down to the studio tomorrow and see if I can clean it up."

Gloria felt a dull wave of disappointment. *This had been our only real chance of finding some evidence to show this wasn't just a prank.* She thought of her parents, how just a few hours earlier they had been sitting around the supper table, laughing and telling stories and feeling like everything was safe and good. *And now this*, she thought.

Gloria wiped a tear from her eye and stood up. "I think I should call my parents," she said. "It's kind of late, but if they hear about this on the news, they'll be upset that I didn't call them. You want to call your mom first, though?"

"Nah," Ashante said. "You go ahead. I think I'm gonna go to bed. It's been an awfully long day."

***

Ashante climbed into bed, but she was too keyed up to sleep. She sometimes wished she had a family like Gloria's. Ashante hadn't called her parents about the cross burning and she didn't plan to. Her mother, who had recently remarried, wasn't interested in Ashante's life at Lakeside.

"You don't need college. What you need is a good man," her mother had told her when Ashante first started asking about schools. She had accused Ashante of 'putting on airs', acting like she was better than the rest of the family. Her mother had even introduced her once as "my educated heifer." Lying there in the dark, Ashante imagined what her mother would say if she had called her tonight. *See, if you'd stayed home, none of this would have ever happened.*

Ashante's father was just too busy, in his own words, to be involved in his grown children's lives. Ashante figured he was afraid she'd ask him for money. Fortunately, she'd cobbled together tuition money with scholarships and loans—in fact, she realized now, it had been a long time since she'd been able to rely on her parents for anything. Her closeness with Tyrone would have to get her through this. Oh, how she wished he was there beside her! She tried to calm herself by softly humming an old gospel song her grandmother used to sing, to help her get through tough times.

Ashante hoped her friend was getting the comfort she needed by calling home. *G.W. is so naive sometimes. I tried telling her this is a hick college, but it had to take something like this for her to believe it,* Ashante thought.

Ashante grew up in a real city. Racial strife and the indifference of the police were just a part of life. One of the reasons she chose Lakeside was because it had a great broadcasting program—and Ashante had always known she belonged behind a microphone. But she'd also picked Lakeside because it was far away from the tension-filled environment she had grown up in. She'd felt comforted by the small-town ways, how everything felt quiet and safe. *That's all changed now*, she thought. She pulled the covers close to her chin. She thought she'd seen some things, back in her old neighborhood, but even she had never dealt with something as serious as a cross burning before.

Ashante closed her eyes and wished it would all go away. As soon as she did, however, images of the burning cross filled her mind. She got up, walked quietly to the bathroom and searched the medicine cabinet. After taking sleeping pills, she crawled back into bed and lay staring at the ceiling, waiting for the medicine to kick in.

***

Meanwhile Gloria made the phone call home.

"Hi, Momma," she said. Before she could say anything more, Gloria burst into tears.

"What on earth?" her mother said. "Gloria-honey, what is it? Are you alright?"

Slowly Gloria told her mother what had happened. The phone call involved everyone as each family member had to hear the details so she repeated the story again and again.

Gloria's father was last. He listened silently as Gloria shared the details, but as soon as she was finished, he made no attempt to hide his outrage, especially at the police.

"It's the same everywhere, baby," he said. "They think if you're black, you're guilty. Your brother got pulled over by the cops a few weeks ago for no reason. He wasn't speeding or anything. They just pulled him over and asked him a bunch of questions. They even made him get out of the car and spread eagle, claiming they had to check him for weapons. When I went to the station to find out why it happened, the cop I talked to used the same exact words, 'you are blowing this all out of proportion.'"

"Why didn't you tell me this before?"

"We didn't want to worry you. Anthony was a little shaken up, but he's fine now. When I was your age, my momma used to remind me that I could be in the right place for the right reason, but that didn't make it right in the white world. I just want you to know this type of thing happens to blacks every day. So don't let anyone make you feel as if it's your fault, baby girl."

Gloria's mother chimed in, from another extension. "Do you want to come home?"

"No, Momma," Gloria said, fighting back tears. "That wouldn't solve anything. Whoever did this would think he won. I've worked too hard here to let something like this ruin it all. Besides, we may have proof."

"What's this about proof?" her father cut in. "What kind of proof?"

She didn't want to tell her parents about the tape, since she wasn't sure what was on it.

"Well, there are some rumors that someone may have seen something. We'll know more tomorrow."

Gloria felt guilty about not telling her parents everything, but she knew they would want her to turn the tape over to the authorities. She couldn't do that until she found someone in power they could trust.

The phone call lasted longer than Gloria expected, and before her mother would let her go, she led Gloria in prayer.

"Honey, turn it over to God, and remember he will never leave your side."

After they said goodbye, Gloria went into the living room and turned off the lights, but she quickly snapped them back on. It had been years since she'd been afraid of the dark, but she couldn't get the image of the flames out of her mind.

Although Gloria was sure she wouldn't be able to sleep, she decided to go to bed, anyway. As she made her way down the dark hallway, her hip banged into the edge of the storage cabinet. She winced and fumbled in the dark until she found the light switch. *Why on earth did Ashante move the cabinet?* she thought. Swearing,

Gloria leaned her weight against the heavy piece of furniture and pushed it back against the wall, by the small door that led up to the unfinished attic. Heavy smudges of dirt in the carpet caught her eye, but she was too tired to clean it up.

For a moment, Gloria thought about leaving the light on, but then she shook her head. "I will not be afraid in my own house," she said firmly and switched off the light.

Feeling bruised and battered, Gloria buried herself under her bed pillows and asked God to give her the strength to get through this ordeal. She lay in bed, trying to focus on something positive, rather than giving into her fears. For some reason, Jamal's face came to mind. She remembered the fury in his eyes as he put out the flames and, later, the intensity in his expression as he condemned the night's events.

"Ashante is right. He is easy to look at," Gloria mumbled as she fell into a restless sleep.

The nightmare started almost immediately. In the dream, Gloria looked out a window into a deep fog, as a bright light drew closer. In the mist she saw a silhouette of a woman nailed to a cross. The word *"nigger"* was stamped on her forehead. She saw figures dressed in white robes. Their taunting was shrill and harsh. She got close enough to see the woman's face. It was Ashante. Gloria looked again, and her own face looked back. She felt like she was burning inside and looked down to see flames surrounding her.

The ringing of the telephone startled Gloria awake.

She grabbed for it with one hand, wiping sweat from her forehead with the other. "Hello?" she said, her heart pounding in her throat.

A male voice answered. "Is this the house where the cross was burned tonight?"

In her sleepy confusion, Gloria thought the caller might be the campus police, finally following up on the crime. "Yes!" she said, relieved. "Who is this?"

"I—I'm not sure why I'm calling. But what they did was terrible," the caller said. "You have to understand that's just how they are. It was nothing personal."

Gloria sat up, instantly alert. But she kept her voice calm, afraid the caller would hang up if she sounded too excited. "You know who did it?" she said.

"I know what I know," the caller replied. "But, that's not why I'm calling. I just wanted you to know it's not like everyone on campus is racist or against black people. Some of us just get caught up in shit and before we know it, it's too late."

"Can you tell me who did it?" Gloria asked.

"It won't do you any good."

"Why not? They committed a crime. They should be expelled. They should be arrested." Gloria heard the urgency in her voice and struggled to control it.

"The university won't do anything," the caller told her. "As far as the police are concerned, this is just a big waste of time."

"Could you at least tell me your name?"

"No way. I've told you more than I should have already. Mea culpa, mea culpa. I gotta go."

And the phone went silent.

Gloria ran to wake up Ashante. She called her name and even shook her, but received no response other than light snoring. Then she noticed the bottle of sleeping pills on the bedside table. She went into the kitchen for some water and drank it slowly as she worked up the courage to look out the front window. A car cruised by, its headlights dimmed, and she recognized the campus patrol car. She felt reassured for a moment, but then her eyes were drawn to the circle of scorched grass where the cross had blazed just hours before. The glow from the streetlights revealed just enough to bring her anger rushing back.

"Why?" she asked aloud. "Why would they do this? Why us?" Her questions reminded her of Sgt. Thomas and his callous attitude.

"I guess we *did* do something to provoke them," she whispered to the night. "We were in the wrong place at the wrong time, with the wrong skin color."

Gloria shivered, even though it was warm inside the house. She couldn't shake the feeling that someone was watching her. Despite her brave words to her parents, she really wished she could go home. She couldn't remember a time when she had been so frightened.

She wrapped her robe tighter and retreated to Ashante's room. She climbed into bed next to Ashante, shivered again, and huddled close to her friend, trying to push her fear away long enough to fall asleep. As the impact of the night's event hit home, she was once again reminded what racism was really like and how much it deeply hurt.

## CHAPTER FOUR

A shante slapped wildly at the alarm clock but the insistent beep continued. Sitting up groggily she realized the phone was ringing. It was only 5:45 a.m. She was surprised to see Gloria beside her in the bed.

"Please tell me last night didn't happen," Ashante groaned. "Is that the phone?"

"I'll get it," Gloria said.

"Whoever it is better have a damn good reason for calling at this ungodly hour," Ashante said as she sank back under the covers.

"Hello?" Gloria said.

"May I speak to Gloria Wilson or Ashante Melashe, please?" a male voice asked.

Gloria steeled herself for yet another prank call. "Who is this?" she said.

The man cleared his throat. "This is Dean Severson, from Lakeside University. It's important that I speak with Gloria or Ashante immediately."

"Oh," Gloria said. "Sorry—this is Gloria."

"Gloria, I'm sorry to be calling so early, but I just heard about the incident at your house last night. How are you and Ashante doing this morning?"

"We're all right, I guess," Gloria mumbled.

"A very unfortunate incident," Severson continued. "I think it would be best for us to meet and discuss it. I would like you and Ashante to come to my office first thing this morning."

"We have classes first thing," Gloria said.

"I'd be happy to talk to your professors and explain your absence."

"Could you hold on a second and let me check with Ashante?"

Gloria quickly told Ashante what the Dean had to say, and they stared at each other, bewildered, tired and frozen in a prolonged silence. Finally, Ashante said, "tell him to at least wait until this afternoon. We need a chance to clean up that tape."

Gloria thought fast, and then returned to the phone. "Dean Severson," she lied, "Ashante has monitoring duty in the campus studio all morning, and it's too late to find a replacement."

Severson sighed. "Very well, we'll make it later in the day, then," he said. "But it is very important that you do not talk to anyone else about the incident until you meet with me."

"Why is that?" Gloria said, an uneasy feeling sinking in.

"We need to go over the events and decide the best course of action," Severson said. "The more people who know about this, the greater the chance of things getting blown out of proportion. Listen, we can discuss this further in my office. What time can you be here?"

Hearing those words again—*blown out of proportion*—made Gloria angry. They needed as much time as possible, she realized, to gather their evidence.

"How about two o'clock?" she finally said.

"I'd prefer to meet with you sooner," Severson said.

"I can't see us getting there before then."

"Very well, two o'clock. I can't stress enough, however, just how important it is that you two not speak to anyone else about this until we meet."

"You've made that pretty clear."

"Then I have your word on that?"

"We'll see you at two, Dean Severson," Gloria said firmly. "Good bye."

Gloria told Ashante about the afternoon appointment with the Dean and then recounted, word for word, her conversation with the mysterious caller the night before.

"Did you recognize the voice? Do you have any idea who it was?" Ashante asked.

"No clue. But he said something strange like, 'my copa, my copa.' At least that's what it sounded like."

"Are you sure?"

"I don't know. I was half-asleep," she said, as she stifled a yawn in the back of her hand.

"So, what do we do now?" Ashante said. "What if the caller was right and the administration just looks the other way? It sounds like Severson wants to keep this quiet."

"We have to get enough evidence so they can't ignore it," Gloria said. "Let's look at what we know so far. The caller said 'they,' so we know there's more than one of them, right?"

Ashante grimaced. "That certainly narrows it down," she said wryly. "But it's a start. The jerk who called about the cross was definitely white. No matter what that cop said. By the way, what did your parents say?"

"They're worried sick. Momma wanted me to come home. Daddy wanted to come up here and talk to the president. Of course Anthony was all ready to come up here and kick some butt." Gloria smiled. "You should call your folks, Ashante."

"I've got enough to deal with right now. I think I'll just stick with calling Tyrone. I still can't believe this is happening."

"Neither can I. Seriously, we're just starting the 21st century! I know I can be gullible, but I never thought I'd have to be worrying about burning crosses in my yard. When are we going to get beyond all of this?"

"I don't know, G.W. Maybe we never will. You want to believe that things have changed and then something like this happens, and you realize we haven't come very far at all. I just can't figure out why we were targeted. Neither one of us is outspoken when it comes to black causes. I haven't had any run-ins with anyone over race, discounting the stares and people being unfriendly at times."

"Same here."

"I'm really scared, which doesn't happen to me often," Ashante said, burrowing deeper under the covers.

"You and me both, girl," Gloria said. "But I'm also stirring inside, and I can hear my momma telling me that no one has the right to make us feel this way. We have to catch whoever did this and make them pay!"

"Alright, G.W., I'm with you, girl," Ashante smiled. "I'll take the tape down to the studio first thing and try to clean it up."

"Great," Gloria said. "See what you can do. It may be our only chance to nail these guys. I'm going to head over to the student newspaper office. I want to get all of this down in an article before we see Severson. Right now it's still fresh in my mind, and I know just what I want to say. Who knows how I'll feel after our meeting."

"Do you think he'd want you to write an article about it?"

"He said not to *talk* to anyone. He didn't say anything about not *writing* about it," Gloria said. "Besides, he won't find out until after it's printed."

"So, I take it this means we're cutting classes today?" Ashante said, with a grin.

## CHAPTER FIVE

After breakfast, the two parted ways at the campus library. Gloria worked on her article all morning. The headline read, *'RACISM EXISTS AS BLACK STUDENTS ARE TERRORIZED BY BURNING CROSS.'* Gloria opened the article by detailing the night's events. She wrote about the fear and helplessness she and Ashante felt when the police claimed it was merely a prank. She wrote, briefly, about the history of cross burnings, and how they had been used for generations to target black communities and instill fear and powerlessness. *'The University must protect its black students,'* Gloria wrote, in closing. *'It cannot look the other way. This act of hatred and racism must be met with appropriate punishment. We must find the culprits and see they never have the opportunity to do this type of thing again.'*

After she finished, she read the story once more all the way through. Her father had always preached the importance of standing up for themselves, of telling their own truth. Gloria had never been in a situation where she thought that lesson mattered more. She knew her momma would rather she come home, but she couldn't help but think her father would be proud that she was choosing to stay and speak out.

She printed off a copy and tracked down the paper's editor, Lori Christianson, in the student lounge.

"Lori," she said, "I have an article I'd like you to consider for the front page of the *Campus Tempo*."

Lori looked relieved and happy to see Gloria and gave her arm a small squeeze. "I heard about what happened at your place last night," she said. "I'm so sorry. Is that what the article is about?"

"Yeah, bad news always travels faster, doesn't it? I wanted to get it all down on paper while it was still fresh. I think I got it the way I want it."

"Do you have any idea who did it?" Lori asked.

"Nothing for sure, but we've got a few leads."

"All right, the editorial board meets later today. I'll run this by them and let you know."

"Thanks, I appreciate it," Gloria said. She glanced at the clock, surprised to see it was already almost 1 p.m. "I gotta go, Lori—I'll catch you later!"

Gloria left the article with Lori and hurried home. Ashante was already there, putting together a quick lunch.

"Hey," Gloria said. "Any progress on the tape? Did you get it cleaned up?"

Ashante shook her head and looked disappointed. "Well, I got started on it, but then someone else needed the equipment. I've got the tape in my purse. I'll finish it up after we talk to Severson, and then we'll see what we've got. How 'bout you? How's your article coming?"

"It's in the hands of the editor, but we'll have to wait until Wednesday for it to run."

"Great," Ashante said. "Oh! I talked to Tyrone."

"I'm so glad you reached him. What did he say?"

"He wanted to take the next flight out, but I told him we'd be all right. He also wanted us to get out of the house. You know that law firm he interned at while he was at Lakeside? He said he would call them and see if we have any legal options at this point." Ashante poured two glasses of water and handed one of them to Gloria. "I also told Tyrone about your conversation with the mystery caller last night, and he said it sounded like Latin—'mea culpa, mea culpa'—which means, 'it's my fault'. G.W., he thought the caller might have been apologizing."

Gloria raised her eyebrows in surprise. "Apologizing? Ashante, do you think the caller was in on it?"

Ashante shook her head. "I wondered the same thing," she said.

"We should probably head to Severson's office," Gloria said. "I'd really hoped we would have more evidence, but I guess we'll have to wing it."

At two o'clock, Gloria and Ashante were ushered in to meet with Dean Severson. The Dean was a short, stocky man with pale, blue eyes. His hair was combed in wisps over his bald spot. He sat behind a mahogany desk, fidgeting with a single piece of paper and looking distracted.

Severson glanced up at the sound of the door. "Gloria, Ashante, please have a seat," he said. "How are you today? I hope you were able to get some sleep last night. I asked Officer Rodriguez to patrol the area around your house."

"Thanks," Gloria said. "I saw him drive by in the middle of the night."

"Well, it's the least we can do," Severson said. "I appreciate you taking the time to meet with me. President Horning and I want to express our concern over what happened. We know we have a serious situation on our hands."

"Then you do agree we need to take action," Gloria said.

"We need to get to the bottom of this," Severson said, "but before we do, I have to ask you a question." Severson wiped his brow and straightened the paper laying on his desk. "Ladies, why didn't you stick to our agreement not to discuss these events with anyone?"

"I don't know what you mean," Gloria said. She glanced in Ashante's direction.

Severson leaned forward, his elbows on the table. "An hour ago, I was handed *this* by President Horning who, I have to tell you, found it very upsetting."

Severson held up the piece of paper—it was a copy of Gloria's article. "How did you find time to write this when you told me you had classes all morning?"

31

Gloria paused and glanced down at her hands. "I thought it would be more effective if I wrote it this morning, rather than waiting and forgetting some of the details," she finally said. "But, how did the president get it? I just gave it to the editor a couple of hours ago!"

"I suspect someone on the editorial board recognized the inflammatory nature of your article and brought it to President Horning."

"Inflammatory?" Gloria lifted her chin. "I just wrote what happened. There was a cross burned in our yard. Isn't that inflammatory?"

"You did much more than simply relate details here," Severson said. He spoke quietly, but firmly. "The *Campus Tempo* is the official voice of this institution, not your personal sounding board. This entire article is laced with your bias on what took place."

Suddenly Ashante, who had barely said a word, leaned forward. "Bias?" she said. "Let me get this straight. You're accusing her of being biased? What about the people who burned that cross?"

"Wait a minute, calm down," Severson said. "That's not what I said. We are investigating, but at this point there is very little to go on. Certainly not enough to warrant such harsh accusations. In your article, Gloria, you claim the school doesn't care about its black students. Now there's nothing farther from the truth. The fact is, this could have been a prank by a few foolish students who got carried away. Do you know how many cars get egged around here? How many trees are toilet-papered by students after a big game? We have to be one hundred percent sure this was racially motivated before we allow this article to be printed."

"I was called a *nigger!*" Ashante said. "Whoever burned that cross knew what they were doing. We were targeted because we are black."

"If that ends up being true," Dean Severson said, "you can be assured we will respond appropriately, but we don't know anything for sure at this point. Until then, it doesn't do anyone any good to escalate this matter."

Ashante shook her head. "We have a tape—," she started to say, but her voice broke off as Gloria shook her head with a look of warning.

"What tape?" Severson asked, his eyes narrowing.

"A tape I made for my broadcasting class," Ashante said, reluctantly. "It has my side of the phone conversation on it. I'm not sure what else, but it may contain something that will help us find out who's responsible."

"Where is this tape now?" Dean Severson asked.

Gloria started to say something, but Ashante was already on the same page.

"The tape's back at the studio," Ashante said, instinctively clutching her purse. "I have to do some more work on it to clear out the background noise so we can hear it better."

"I'd like that tape," Dean Severson said.

"What for?" Gloria said.

"If there's anything on it of value, then it qualifies as evidence. It needs to be turned over to the police."

"The police aren't going to do anything," Gloria said. "They made that perfectly clear last night."

"I'm sure that isn't true," Dean Severson said. "Besides, the campus police are now handling the investigation, and I assure you they will conduct it in a thorough and professional manner. In the meantime, you two will only make the situation worse if you insist on withholding evidence. I'd like that tape. As for the article, I've informed the editor not to publish it."

"You can't do that!" Gloria said, jumping to her feet.

"I already did. We reserve the right to exercise editorial license, you know that."

"There's a big difference between editorial license and censorship!" Gloria said.

"The subject is closed. Trust me. We'll handle this situation. You need to let us do our job. Am I making myself clear?"

Gloria stared back at Severson, speechless.

Ashante reached over and placed her hand on Gloria's arm. "You're crystal clear," Ashante said. "Let's go, G.W. This isn't getting us anywhere."

"This isn't right," Gloria said. She shook with indignation as Ashante pulled her out the door. When they were out of earshot of the Dean, Gloria turned to Ashante. "Can you believe that?" she said.

"Don't let him get under your skin. We still have the tape. I'm sorry I blabbed about it. I wasn't thinking. I'm going to work on clearing up the sound, even if it takes me all day. Wanna come?"

"No, you go on. I want to go talk to the campus cops. If they have any leads on who was prowling around our place last week, it may bring us a step closer to whoever burned that cross."

"Good idea. Meet you back at the apartment?"

"I'll probably go for a walk by the lake afterwards. I need some time to unwind."

"Okay, catch you later, sister. And be safe."

## CHAPTER SIX

The Campus Police Station sat on the edge of the university grounds, a squat building made of cinder block. Inside, the fluorescent lights cast a greenish glow on the rows of old metal desks. A handful of officers filled the room, answering the phones and filling out paperwork. No one looked up when Gloria stepped up to the empty reception desk.

She scanned the room, looking for Officer Carlos Rodriguez. He was the one who'd taken their report after Ashante saw the prowler looking in their window. Gloria recognized him now and approached his desk.

He looked up. "Can I help you?"

"I hope so. I'm Gloria Wilson. I was hoping I could talk with you."

Officer Rodriguez looked around. Then he stood up and nodded toward an empty conference room. "Sure," he said. "Let's go talk in there."

"I have some questions," Gloria said, once they'd sat down.

But Officer Rodriguez frowned. "I don't really have any new information," he said. "I spent the night patrolling your house, but I didn't see anything out of the ordinary."

"Severson did mention that he asked you to keep an eye on things," she said. "Thank you for that. But actually I wanted to ask you about the prowler report we filed earlier."

Rodriguez looked uncomfortable. "That prowling incident touched some nerves around here," he said. "It would be better if you just forgot about it. Look at it as no harm done."

"I don't understand," Gloria said.

"To be honest, neither do I," Rodriguez replied. "After I took your report about the prowlers, I started keeping an eye on your place. The next night, I noticed two guys slinking around in the back alley. I asked them a few questions—their excuse for being there was pretty lame, something about looking for a place to rent, but I couldn't hold them on that alone." Rodriguez paused and frowned again. "Anyway, I filed a report. Next thing I knew, the Chief of Security was in my office, telling me to get rid of the report and that the whole thing never happened."

Gloria stared at Rodriguez in disbelief. "Why would he do that?"

"That's what I can't figure out. I got the feeling someone a little further up the ladder was leaning on him to keep those guys' names out of the spotlight."

"Who were they?"

"I'm sorry. I can't tell you that. Because the report no longer exists, the incident technically never occurred. I wish I could help you, but I've probably already told you more than I should have."

Gloria nodded, indicating that she understood. Officer Rodriguez seemed like he meant what he was saying. She wondered if she'd found the one authority figure on campus who could be trusted. "The thing is," Gloria said, they're probably the ones who burned the cross."

"Whoa, now," Rodriguez said, glancing toward the closed conference room door. "There's no evidence what they were up to that night, much less anything that ties them to the cross burning. I'm just telling you that you'll be stepping on some pretty powerful toes if you keep asking questions."

"Do you really think it's just a coincidence?"

"Maybe, maybe not. Let me look into it, okay?"

"How do I know you will? The Westport cops certainly weren't very helpful."

Rodriguez paused, and Gloria thought she saw something flash in his eyes. "You called the Westport cops?" he said.

"No, they just showed up. Started asking questions and making it sound like the whole thing was our fault."

"Do you remember the officers' names?"

"Um, Sgt. Thomas and Sgt. Carlson."

"Those two," Rodriguez muttered, shaking his head.

"You know them?"

"Yeah," Rodriguez said. "Let's leave it at that."

"But why weren't you the one at our house last night?" Gloria said. "Isn't that your beat?"

Rodriguez nodded. "I was on my way, but the dispatcher sent me to another call—a break-in on the other side of campus. It turned out to be a false alarm. I'll look into it now, though, especially since Thomas and Carlson are involved." He paused, and Gloria found herself wanting to believe him. "Look," he continued, "I'll personally patrol your area for the next couple of weeks. You have my word. I was raised to believe that a person is only as good as his word, so that's sacred to me."

With a smile he added, "Now, how 'bout you get out of here and let me get back to work."

Gloria smiled, and they both stood up. "Thank you," Gloria said.

"Just doing my job," Rodriguez said.

***

Rodriguez watched Gloria walk away, and realized he had divulged too much information. He glanced around, relieved to see that none of his fellow cops seemed to have noticed who Gloria was.

He couldn't help it, though. Gloria reminded him so much of Maria, a victim he'd tried to help at his last job in Milwaukee. Both Gloria and Maria had the same earnest look about them, the same eager attitude. Back in Milwaukee, he had arrested Maria's ex-boyfriend for violating a restraining order. Maria called the station, asking to be informed when Paul was released from jail, but

Rodriquez wasn't able to reach her in time. As soon as he left the jail, Paul broke into Maria's house. If the neighbors hadn't heard her screams, she would probably be dead.

Rodriguez took Maria's assault personally and went off track for nearly a year. He drank excessively and didn't care about himself or the job. It was Maria who helped him sober up and regain his sense of purpose. He would never forget the moment she confronted him.

"It's time for you to stop blaming yourself and get on with your life," she said. "You didn't beat me—it wasn't your fault, now forgive yourself!"

He had wept like a baby afterwards. He hadn't taken a drink since that day, and he had sworn he would provide as much information as he could to future victims.

But he hadn't told Gloria one crucial piece of information: that he was no stranger to Thomas and Carlson. He'd worked with them back when he was a rookie in Milwaukee and had witnessed their warped level of corruption up close. When Thomas and Carlson were suspended for stealing drugs from the Evidence Room, they tried to pin the theft on him.

It took him thousands of dollars and a painful internal investigation to clear his name. And though all of the charges were eventually dropped, he vowed to bring Thomas and Carlson to justice some day.

When Rodriguez learned the two had landed jobs in Westport, he put in for a transfer, knowing one day they were sure to slip up.

***

Gloria left the police station and headed for the crystal blue lake on the west edge of campus. Maple, birch and a sprinkling of oak trees hugged parts of the shoreline, butting up against an expansive meticulously manicured lawn. In the warmer months, students played volleyball here, sunned on the lawn, and colored the entire lake in rented canoes.

But today, Gloria had the lake to herself. She walked along the worn pathway that wove through the trees, and watched as the luminous lake reflected the early autumn sun. A pair of mallard ducks paddled near the edge of the water. She sat down under a maple tree and watched the ducks swim close. This was her favorite place for escape when she needed to collect her thoughts. She came here often.

Today, though, the soothing effects of nature failed to work its magic. She thought about what Rodriguez had shared with her and her mind started racing. Each new piece of information seemed to compound the others—the burning cross, the cops' attitudes, the mysterious caller's message, the administration's reaction, and now Officer Rodriguez's warning. Who could have wanted their report destroyed? Who were the police protecting? Looking out across the wide expanse of the lake, Gloria felt very, very small. Suddenly, she heard someone calling her name.

She looked up and saw Ashante running towards her down the path, a frantic look on her face.

"Someone took it!" Ashante shouted. "It's gone! They took it right out of my purse!"

"Slow down!" Gloria said, climbing to her feet. "What do you mean?"

"The tape! I had it with me in my purse, and now it's gone!"

"But, how? When?"

Ashante paused to catch her breath. "After I left you, I cut through the Union on my way to the studio. I saw Chuck, and we stopped to talk, and I set my purse down. I wasn't even there a half hour. When I got to the studio, the tape was gone."

"Are you sure you had it in your purse?"

"Positive. I checked right after we left Severson's office."

"That doesn't make any sense. The only person we told about the tape was Severson. And as low as my opinion of him is right now, I honestly can't believe he would stoop to robbing purses!"

Ashante glanced at the ground. "Well, I did tell some other people about the tape," Ashante said.

"You did what? Who?"

"Some of the guys at the studio, and a couple of friends," Ashante said. "Everyone kept asking about what happened and guessing who could have done it! I just wanted them to know that we were doing something about it, so I told them about the tape."

"Oh, Ashante," Gloria groaned covering her face with her hands.

"God, I'm so stupid," Ashante said, her eyes filling with tears. "I've ruined everything, haven't I?"

"No, no, you're not stupid. You had no way of knowing someone would steal it. Think, though. Did you see anyone near your purse while you were at the Union?"

"It was so crowded in there. You know how it is at that time of day. I didn't really pay any attention."

Gloria sighed, trying to make this piece of information fit with all the others. The destroyed police report. The canceled article. The stolen tape. It all added up, she knew—but into what?

She tried to give Ashante a consoling look. "At least we know we've got them worried," Gloria said. "They must think there was something really incriminating on that tape to risk stealing it."

"Yeah, but if they were willing to do that, what else might they try?"

They hugged each other tightly and headed home. No place felt safe right now.

## CHAPTER SEVEN

When they got home, Gloria sank to the couch. "We need to decide what to do next about the tape," she told Ashante, "but I need to take a break first and try to clear my mind. That okay with you?"

Ashante nodded. "Me, too," she said. "I'm going to tidy up around here and try to distract myself."

Gloria thumbed through the morning's edition of *The Herald*, Westport's daily newspaper—until her eyes landed on a headline, buried on the next-to-last page. It was a tiny article barely a couple of paragraphs long. The headline read, *Cross Burning Termed Prank by LU Officials*.

Gloria quickly skimmed the article, sputtering with rage. "Ashante!" she shouted, over the hum of the vacuum cleaner. "Listen to this!"

"Now what?" Ashante asked, as the vacuum rumbled to a stop.

Gloria read the beginning of the article out loud. "'*A burning cross reported Sunday night in the front yard of a house rented by two Lakeside University students has been termed a college prank by LU officials. Witnesses saw the flames around 10:30 p.m. but failed to see anyone leaving the scene. No damage occurred, and there were no injuries. According to President David Horning, the incident was not racially-oriented, but rather an unfortunate prank.*'"

"That's bullshit!" Ashante exclaimed, peering over Gloria's shoulder.

"They're not going to look into it at all," Gloria said. "They've already dismissed it as nothing." She crumpled the newspaper and flung it across the floor. "Oh, this just gets better and better!"

"I can't believe the newspaper is in on this cover-up, too," Ashante said. "Surely the newspaper people can see there is a bigger story here. They had a reporter on the scene fast enough.

He was snapping pictures left and right and asking everyone questions."

"I know," Gloria said with a wry smile. "He was in my face right before I threw up all over the driveway."

"So what happened? Where are all his photos?"

"I don't know. It looks like I'm not the only reporter whose story didn't make it to press today."

"Jesus. Somebody really does have a lot of influence," Ashante said. "To influence a daily newspaper takes a lot of pull."

Gloria thought about what Rodriguez had said. *You'll be stepping on some pretty powerful toes.* She turned to her roommate. "Ashante, what have we gotten ourselves into?"

For a long moment, neither of them spoke. Outside, a car drove by, its headlights briefly illuminating the windows.

"Hey, by the way," Ashante said. "What did you track all over the hallway last night? There was gross crud all over the hallway."

Gloria looked up. "I didn't track that in. I thought you did," she said. "I saw it last night on my way to bed."

"Well, I didn't track it in, either. I was barefoot last night, and those were definitely big, muddy shoeprints."

"Wait a minute," Gloria said. "You're sure it was shoeprints?"

"Yeah, why?"

"I didn't even go down the hall until I was on my way to bed." Gloria's eyes widened. "That means someone else was in our hallway!"

"And those voices we heard on the tape!" Ashante said. "Those weren't from the crowd outside—they were inside our house!"

"And we just vacuumed up the evidence," Gloria said quietly.

"I did it again!" Ashante said. "First the tape, and now this."

"It's not your fault. I would have cleaned it up last night, but I was too tired. But we should check to see if anything's missing."

They searched every room in the house, but everything appeared to be exactly where it was supposed to be. They sank back onto the couch, worried and confused.

Gloria felt defeated. Whatever they were up against, it was just too big and powerful. "Maybe we shouldn't stay here anymore," she said. "What if they come back? Maybe Momma is right, and we'd be safer staying someplace else."

"No," Ashante said. "I'm not going to be terrorized into leaving. This is our place, Gloria! Look at all the work we've put into fixing it up. I'm scared, too. But we can't let whoever did this force us out. Rodriguez is patrolling. We don't even know for sure who left those shoeprints. And you know, maybe that cop left the prints. He used the bathroom, remember?"

Gloria sat up straight, as something occurred to her. "Wait, Ashante. Come to think of it, maybe he didn't use the bathroom. He must not have flushed because I never heard the pipes vibrate. Did you?"

Ashante shook her head. "No! If he wasn't using the john, what was he doing?"

"I have no idea," Gloria said.

"The longer this goes on, the more paranoid I feel. I hate feeling this way."

Gloria nodded. "Me, too," she said. She was about to say more when the phone rang. "I'll get it," Gloria said. "I don't want to feel terrorized, either. And I certainly don't want to feel afraid every time the phone rings." She gave Ashante's arm a squeeze, then hurried to the kitchen to answer the phone. "Hello?"

"Hi, this is Jamal. May I speak with Gloria?"

"Hey, it's me," Gloria said, surprised he would call.

"Word is you and your roommate had a meeting with the Dean today," Jamal said. "How'd that go?"

Gloria told him all about their confrontation with the Dean, including the suppression of her article.

"It's just what I expected," he fumed.

Gloria told him about the article in *The Herald*, but kept quiet about the stolen tape and about her conversation with Officer Rodriguez. "So what do we do if the administration is covering for these guys?" she asked.

"We make so much noise that they can't ignore us. We have to let our voices be heard. We have to let the whole community know this was a racist attack and that we're not going to stand by and take it."

"What do you have in mind?"

"I've scheduled a BSO meeting tomorrow to discuss what happened and to demand an investigation from university officials," Jamal said. "That's why I called, actually—to see if you and Ashante can be there. It's at seven-thirty tomorrow night in the Union."

"I can be there, and I'll tell Ashante," Gloria said.

"Great. If you want, you can read your article. They can't very well censor that," Jamal said. "See you then." He hung up without even saying good-bye.

Gloria turned and walked quickly back to the living room. She shouldn't be excited that Jamal had called—after all, he only wanted to talk to her because of what had happened on their lawn. Still, Gloria couldn't help but feel a little excited that now Jamal knew her name.

"Who was that?" Ashante asked.

Gloria suppressed a smile. "Jamal," she said.

"Ooh! Hot date?"

"Yeah right! No, he wants us to attend the Black Student Organization meeting tomorrow night. Can you go?"

"Absolutely."

The phone rang again.

"It's like Grand Central Station around here!" Gloria grumbled, rushing back to the kitchen. This time, Ashante followed her.

"Hello?" Gloria said.

"May I speak to Gloria or Ashante?"

"This is Gloria."

"Hey, this is Bruce Saxton, student body president. How are you?"

"Okay, I guess."

"Well listen, the reason I'm calling is I heard about what happened at your place last night. The whole campus is talking about it, and there are a lot of nasty rumors flying around. I figured the best way to calm things down was to call a meeting of all the student organizations. Hopefully we can get to the bottom of this and come up with a solution."

"Something definitely needs to be done," Gloria agreed.

"That's why I think we need to take this to the student body as a whole. I got the auditorium in the Barton Center reserved for Friday night at eight. Can you and your roommate make it? We'd like you to tell everyone what happened."

"Friday night? All right," Gloria said. "I'm not much for speaking in front of people, though. Ashante might be a better speaker."

Ashante shook her head fervently. Gloria sighed. "I guess I could do it," she said.

"We don't need a formal speech or anything," Bruce said. "Just tell us what happened. See you then."

As Gloria hung up, Ashante started to laugh. "If this keeps up, we won't need dates anymore. We'll be spending all our time in meetings and rallies! How's that for a new normal?"

Gloria gave a weak smile and shook her head. "I don't think anything will ever be back to normal," she said. "My momma would say there ain't no normal life for black folks—there's just coping."

## CHAPTER EIGHT

The next night, Gloria and Ashante arrived at the BSO meeting a few minutes early. Of the 70 black students at Lakeside, almost all of them came out and squeezed into the small meeting room. As they waited for the meeting to start, Gloria watched Jamal pacing near the podium. He was GQ handsome, with intense black eyes and neatly trimmed hair. His clean-shaven face made him look boyish, and his reserved, serious demeanor was backed up by his clothes: neatly pressed pants; a crisp, cream-colored shirt; and a bow tie.

Gloria felt Ashante elbow her in the arm. "What?" Gloria whispered.

Ashante grinned and nodded in Jamal's direction. "You know what," she said.

"Stop it," Gloria said, rolling her eyes.

Jamal called the meeting to order and immediately launched into his message, his eyes flashing with emotion, his voice strong and sure.

"By now most of you know what happened Sunday night," Jamal began. "What you may not know, however, is that things are snowballing and this campus is on the brink of a racial crisis. What started with some bigots striking a match is now burning out of control.

The administration would love to cover this up and pretend it never happened. It's our job to make sure they don't get away with it. That's the only way we can make sure this type of thing won't happen again at Lakeside. I've asked Gloria Wilson, one of the victims, to say a few words to you tonight. Come on up here Sister. Show her some love."

The sweat trickled down Gloria's neck as she stood up and made her way to the podium. She grasped the wooden edge to hide her nervousness. *I have a hard time just making small talk*, she thought. *What am I doing, standing up here giving a speech?* She looked around the room at the expectant faces and swallowed hard. She heard her momma's voice, "stand tall and speak from the heart." Taking a deep breath, she began.

"My name is Gloria Wilson. My roommate, Ashante Melashe, and I were called into the Dean's office yesterday, and believe me, it was not so he could commend us for our good grades." The audience let out a ripple of laughter, as Gloria felt herself begin to relax.

"Basically what the Dean wanted was to shut us up and to tell us to leave the investigating to the authorities," she continued. "That's not a bad idea, except the authorities aren't doing much of anything."

"I don't know if any of you saw Monday's edition of *The Herald*. The article about the cross burning was easy to miss. It was buried on the next-to-last page. It stated that city police had turned the investigation over to the campus police. As far as we know the city police never even filed a report. I think the administration's only concern is that this will cast the college in a bad light and affect their financial backing."

"It's the same old, same old, sister," someone shouted out.

Gloria nodded. Her voice now was loud and strong. "The article in *The Herald* also quoted the administration as saying this whole thing was just a harmless prank that should be forgotten," she said. "I can tell you, Dean Severson and President Horning are doing everything in their power to make sure that happens."

By now, the audience hung on every word, and Gloria's nervousness melted away.

"I wrote an article about the cross burning for this week's issue of *Campus Tempo*, but you won't find it on the front page where it belongs. In fact, you won't find it in the paper at all. I gave my article to Lori Christianson, the editor, yesterday afternoon and it was on Horning's desk within an hour."

Angry voices rumbled throughout the room.

"That's not right! It's censorship!"

"Amen, sister!"

"They're always trying to keep us from speaking our minds."

"That's right, that's right!"

"Where do they get off thinking they can just cover this up?"

"Tell it like it is, girl!"

The outbursts continued, increasing in volume, until Jamal raised his hand and called for silence, nodding at Gloria to continue.

"So, it appears it's up to us to see that justice is done," she said. "The problem is, there isn't much solid evidence to go on, as the cops call it. We had two things we thought we could use as evidence; unfortunately one of them was stolen, and the other was accidentally destroyed."

"What kind of evidence?" someone shouted.

"I'd rather not say. We want to keep those responsible guessing," Gloria said. "In the meantime, Ashante and I are working on finding more evidence. What's important is that we keep the pressure on. We all know it wasn't just a harmless prank, and we can't let it be dismissed as one. I don't know why we were chosen as targets, but I do know we're going to do all we can to catch whoever did this, no matter what the administration does or doesn't do."

"Lead the way sister," a voice in the front row shouted. "We're with you."

The room erupted with applause and cheers as Gloria sat down.

"Well, now you see what we're facing," Jamal told his audience. "So, are you ready to take some action?"

"Hell, yeah," the students answered in one voice.

"Are we going to let our sisters be terrorized in their homes?" Jamal asked, his voice rising.

"Hell, no!" the students shouted back.

"Are we going to let the administration cover this up?"

"Hell, no!" The students were on their feet now, fervor lighting their faces.

Jamal was in his element, the seriousness of the situation reflected by the tension in his body and the look of utter concentration on his face. From her vantage point, Gloria was struck again by how handsome he was, a thought that embarrassed her with its irrelevance at the moment.

When the room quieted down, Jamal outlined his plan. He proposed a series of rallies aimed at forcing the administration into conducting a thorough investigation.

"We need to keep this in the forefront until we can gather enough evidence to nail the racists responsible for burning that cross," Jamal said. "That way, the issue will still be hot and we can force the university to take action. It's not going to be easy. If the rumors are true, we're up against not only the administration, but some wealthy big shots, too. You know the saying: 'Money talks and bullshit walks.' Well, this time we're going to talk louder and take no bullshit. Are you all with me on this?"

"Yes!" the students shouted, jumping to their feet once more.

"Okay. I think we need to set the first rally for this Saturday," Jamal said. "That doesn't give us much time to get organized but we've got to cook while the stove's hot. We need signs and leaflets and people to speak. It's important that we look organized, not just a bunch of students shouting for no reason."

"We'll hold the rally outside the administration offices. Normally there wouldn't be anyone around on a Saturday, but for once we have luck on our side. The board of trustees meets this weekend. They're meeting at 10 o'clock, so I suggest we start the rally at nine-thirty. That way we'll be the first thing they see as they arrive."

With those details set, Jamal wrapped things up, giving the students tasks to complete for the rally. Then he approached Gloria and Ashante.

"We really need one of you to speak at the rally to give power to our truth," he told them.

"Not me," Ashante said hastily. "Public speaking is not my scene. I'd stutter and stammer so much, no one would be able to understand me. I'm okay behind a microphone in the studio where I can't see my audience, but face-to-face is a whole different thing. I'll stick with making banners and shouting slogans."

"What about you?" Jamal asked Gloria.

"Oh, I don't know."

"Come on G.W., you'll be great, girl," Ashante urged. "Look at how well it went tonight."

"You were quite effective," Jamal agreed. "And we really do need someone to give a first-hand account."

Gloria looked from Ashante to Jamal and sighed. "Oh, all right," she said.

"Thank you, my sister," Jamal said. "I'll see you later. I've got to catch a few more people before they leave."

As they watched him walk away, Ashante once more nudged Gloria with her elbow. "I'm telling you G.W., that brother is together," she said. "Maybe you should ask him to help you with your speech. You know, long hours, late at night, just the two of you."

"I don't think so," Gloria said, still looking in the direction of Jamal's retreating form. "Jamal has more important things on his mind. Besides, I'm sure he's got plenty of women dying to spend time with him. Why would he bother with me?"

"Why do you always sell yourself short?" Ashante asked, "Any guy would be lucky to have you."

"Well, you don't see them beating down my door, do you?"

"Maybe if you didn't spend so much time with your nose buried in your books, Jamal would notice what a cute nose it is!" Ashante said. "Did you ever think of that?"

"Yes mother," Gloria answered. "Any other advice? Want to tell me how to dress? Remind me to eat my vegetables?"

"Okay, okay, I get the hint. I just want you to be happy."

"Maybe when all of this is over," Gloria said, giving Ashante a quick hug. "Sorry for snapping at you. I know you're just trying to help. I should listen to you more."

"Well, all right! How about if we start with your wardrobe?" Ashante grinned.

"Hey, my clothes are fine!" Gloria said, punching Ashante on the arm.

"Yeah, *Good* gave them away and you *Will* take them!" Ashante giggled, dodging another punch.

## CHAPTER NINE

The next morning Gloria took a shortcut through the Union to get to her Chemistry class. Lining the wide hallway were overstuffed couches and chairs where groups of students hung out between classes. As she walked by, Gloria couldn't help but feel like the chatter quieted and all the faces turned in her direction. She felt her cheeks burn. *I hate being* that *girl*, she thought, as she hurried up to avoid their stares.

For the rest of the week, Gloria avoided the Union. She and Ashante divided their time between class and home; they kept the doors and windows locked and tried not to jump every time the phone rang. Every night, Gloria's mother called and asked if she wanted to come home. Each night, Gloria said no. The BSO meeting had energized her; "I have a purpose in all of this," she told her parents. She looked forward to the student assembly at the end of the week with a mix of excitement and nerves.

Friday night's meeting drew a swelling crowd, packed with members of every student organization on campus. Gloria watched the crowd from her seat in the front row. She wondered if it was curiosity or commitment that drew such large numbers, but she reminded herself that she was no longer the gullible person from just a few days ago.

Bruce Saxton called the meeting to order right on time. Bruce was a balding student in his thirties who sported a ponytail and a home-grown beard. Everybody on campus knew his story: After serving in the Peace Corps for two years, he had reached a dead end in his quest for his life's meaning, and he thought he might find some answers by returning to college. His wide range of experiences had helped him win the student government election by a landslide. And his promise to keep the student union open all night on weekends hadn't hurt, either. He had good rapport with students of color, and his black friends called him either a 'blue-eyed soul brother' or a 'brother from another mother.'"

Bruce invited Gloria to the stage. She was nervous as she made her way to the podium and recounted the events of the past week. She was surprised to see that the white students seemed equally outraged by the Dean's efforts to hush things up.

"This isn't just an issue that affects black students at Lakeside. It affects every one of you," Gloria told her audience. "If they can keep me from expressing my views, they can do it to you, too. Lakeside is going to be your alma mater. It's going to be on your resume. Do you really want your alma mater to be a university with a reputation as a breeding ground for racism and hatred? I know I don't."

The students nodded and shouted their encouragement. Their warm response boosted Gloria's confidence and she quickly felt more at ease. She announced the BSO rally set for the next day and was inspired to see so many white students nodding in agreement, eager to sign up to help.

Bruce Saxton stood up, quickly capturing the students' energy.

"This is something that calls for action from the entire student body," he said. "I think we need to show a united front." He turned to Gloria. "Tell Jamal we're behind him all the way. We'll see him tomorrow morning."

\*\*\*

Saturday dawned bright and sunny. The air felt crisp, and the leaves were starting to show the first touches of color. In his apartment, Jamal paced the floor, eager for the day's events to begin.

"You're going to wear holes in the carpet, dog," his roommate, Kwame Brooks, told him. "It's not normal to have that much energy this early. Sit down, man. You're making me nervous."

"Sorry. I'm good to go," Jamal said, dropping onto the sofa. "I can't wait to see the look on those trustees' faces when they get out of their caddies and find themselves in the middle of a demonstration."

"Yep, I'll bet there'll be a lot of dropped jaws over this one," Kwame said. "I just hope they don't bring out the dogs and fire hoses."

"At least that would get the media's attention."

"You volunteer for the front lines if you want, brother, but I ain't taking no police baton to the head just to get on TV!"

"If it would help draw attention to what's happening here I would," Jamal said quietly.

"Man, that sounds like Martin speaking, not Malcolm."

"Whatever. I just hope Gloria tells it like it is," Jamal told him.

Kwame grinned. "Yeah, what's up with that, anyway?"

"With what?"

"With Gloria, man. You planning to make a play there or what?"

"A play? Hell, no." Jamal said. "What would give you that idea?"

"Relax chief. I just thought, you know, she's pretty fly and since you're in between women right now..."

"If I need you to hook me up, I'll be sure to let you know." Jamal grabbed his jacket and headed for the door. "Come on, get your ass movin'."

Jamal and Kwame arrived at the rally site and waited. It didn't take long for the students to gather. BSO members walked through the crowd, passing out homemade signs. Jamal looked up when Kwame nudged his arm. "Hey," Kwame said, "your girlfriend just got here." Jamal rolled his eyes and watched as Gloria and Ashante approached.

"Hey," Gloria said, then quickly glanced at her feet.

Jamal noticed Ashante stifle a grin as she turned to him. "Looks like a great turn-out," Ashante said. "There must be hundreds of people here!"

Jamal nodded. "I guess Bruce Saxton's as good as his word," he said. He looked out across the campus lawn and recognized representatives from almost every student organization already present. Many of them had brought their own signs and banners that said things like, "No to cross burnings," "No to Censorship," "End to Racism," "Punish the Bigots," "Prejudice is not a Prank," and "Quit Stonewalling."

Jamal looked satisfied. "I think we're really going to show them this time," he said.

When the crowd saw Gloria and Ashante, they broke into a cheer and started chanting: "No more cover-ups! We want justice! No more cover-ups! We want justice!" They waved their signs and punched the air with their fists.

Jamal turned to Gloria and Ashante. "Looks like it's show time," he said.

Jamal let the chanting build to a fevered pitch as he made his way to the top of the administrative building steps. After surveying the crowd, he raised his hands for silence.

He placed the megaphone to his lips so his voice would carry to the far edges of the crowd. "Thank you for coming," he said. "My name is Jamal Washington, and I am the president of Lakeside's Black Student Organization. Racism doesn't affect just students of color—it affects everyone. We need to make our voices heard—the more of us, the better. And it gives me hope to see so many of you here. Now I'd like to turn this over to Bruce Saxton, student government president, for a few words of welcome."

Bruce jogged up the steps. "Thanks man," he said, accepting Jamal's outstretched hand.

Bruce held the megaphone up, and his voice echoed across the crowd. "This rally was a great idea. Demonstration is the key to the people's power. We all know why we're here. We need to call attention to everything that's been happening at Lakeside, and we need to do it in a big way."

"As I said at our meeting last night, this is everybody's problem. Whoever burned that cross made all of us look bad. The only way we can rectify that is to find the people responsible and pressure the administration to take action. In a few minutes, the Board of Trustees will be arriving for their monthly meeting. That's their job. Our job is to raise hell. So let's make as much noise as possible."

The crowd broke into a roar.

"No more cover-ups! We want justice!" Bruce shouted into the megaphone.

"No more cover-ups!" the crowd shouted back.

As the chant continued, Jamal spotted the first car pulling up to the curb, a sleek, black BMW. Jamal motioned for Bruce to hand over the megaphone. "Look!" Jamal shouted above the noise. "Here they come!"

As the first trustee emerged from the BMW, the students increased their volume. Jamal watched as the man stopped and gawked, a stunned expression spreading across his face.

"We want justice!" Jamal shouted into the megaphone.

"No more cover-ups!" the crowd shouted back.

Jamal grinned as the trustee quickly ducked back inside his car.

The chanting continued as President Horning and Dean Severson drove up. Jamal watched as they climbed from their cars and consulted angrily with one another in the parking lot. At the sight of their waving arms and obvious distress, the crowd broke into a fevered pitch.

By now, most of the trustees had arrived. They gathered around Horning and Severson and glanced nervously in the students' direction.

Jamal held up his hands again, and the crowd quieted. Holding the megaphone to his lips, his kept his gaze on the group of mostly men clumped together in the parking lot. He addressed his words to them.

"On Sunday night a cross was burned in the yard of two Lakeside students," he said. "This was not, contrary to our administration's view, a harmless prank. It was a blow directed at every African American on this campus. It may be easy for the President and the Dean to sit in their offices and say this was a harmless prank. But the cross wasn't burning in their yard. They don't have to live with hatred and discrimination every day. They don't understand. But what's even worse is that they don't want to understand. They want to cover this up. They don't want us here today. They want us to shut up and pretend this never happened." He paused and looked out across the crowd. "Well," he shouted to the students, "we're not going to do that, are we?"

"Hell no!" the students yelled back.

"No debate—investigate!" Jamal hollered. The crowd took up the chant, as Severson and Horning hurried across the lawn toward the administration building. The two administrators cringed as they wove through the crowd, then rushed up the steps. Once they reached the top, they stopped and cast angry glances at Jamal.

"You shouldn't be here," Severson blustered, his face only inches from Jamal's.

"Catch the assholes who are responsible and we'll gladly go away," Jamal shouted, using the megaphone so everyone could hear. The students cheered and resumed their chant. "No debate, investigate!"

Jamal turned back to Severson. "Since you're here, Dean, maybe you'd want to share with us why you felt it was necessary to ax Gloria's article. And while you're at it, why don't you share your views on censorship?"

Jamal offered the megaphone to Severson, but the Dean pushed it aside.

"You're way out of line, Mr. Washington," Severson said.

"No sir," Jamal answered. "You're out of line. And you, President Horning, where do you get off, dismissing this as a harmless prank without even investigating?"

Horning was pushing sixty, with coarse white hair trimmed in a close crew cut. His large nose had turned spotty and red from his lost attempts to curb his anger. Even though Jamal was just at six feet tall, Horning towered over him by at least four inches. Horning took the megaphone from Jamal and tried to calm himself as he appealed to the crowd.

"Students, you have the right to demonstrate," Horning said, "but it really isn't necessary. Even as I speak, the campus police are investigating the incident. The Dean and I are working closely with them to find the person or persons responsible." The crowd began to groan, but Horning continued. "As far as the article for the campus newspaper, we decided it served no purpose and would only make the situation worse. Now, I suggest you all go home. You've made your point; now let the investigation run its course."

Horning then turned to lead the trustees into the building. The students resumed their chanting, but they were more subdued.

Jamal grabbed the megaphone, sensing the change in the crowd's mood. "Words, that's all they were," he said. "Just lip service. There's no action to back it up. Take my word for it. Nothing is being done. They don't have to do anything. After all, it was just a harmless prank aimed at a couple of black girls, right? Wrong! I believe the administration knows this was much more than a simple prank, yet they are refusing to take action. We can't let them get away with that. We must be heard!"

The students rose up again with applause, signs and waving banners. A roar from the crowd drew Jamal's attention to a window above his head. Two of the trustees were looking down at the demonstrators. Jamal hurriedly led the students in a new chant: "No more delays! We want action now!"

As the faces disappeared from the window, Jamal took advantage of the lull to present Gloria to the crowd. This time she was not nervous. As she detailed the cross burning, the cops' handling of the incident, and the administration's efforts to cover it up, she was pleased to see the sympathetic looks turn to outrage on most of the faces.

"I'm not here asking for sympathy. I'm asking for justice," Gloria said. "It's okay to feel sorry about what happened, but that won't stop it from happening again. I need help from all of you to find the people responsible and to make sure they face the consequences. I used to think of Lakeside as my home away from home. For the past week, though, I have felt like an outsider. I search every face I pass for the hatred and anger that must be at the root of this act. My roommate jumps every time the phone rings. We both check and recheck the locks on our doors and windows. It's frightening and I'm tired of being frightened." Gloria scanned the crowd and saw Ashante at the very front, nodding and smiling; they locked eyes for a second, and Ashante flashed Gloria a thumbs up.

"The only way to take this fear away," Gloria continued, "to turn this around, is to get justice. I'm also frightened by the administration's indifference. I never thought I'd find this at Lakeside. It sickens me. This is one time when we cannot—we must not—turn the other cheek. This must not be allowed to become yet another case where the authorities look the other way just because we're black."

Gloria paused, copying Jamal's technique in gauging the students' reaction to her words.

"Will you help?" she asked confidently.

"Yes!" the students roared, and the signs waved once more.

The rally ended soon after, but not before another demonstration was set for the following Tuesday. As they left, Jamal asked Gloria if she had noticed any reporters from the local media there.

"No, not that I saw," she said. "After the way the article in *The Herald* was handled on Monday, I think it's obvious someone pretty powerful doesn't want this making headlines. Whoever it is probably has that same influence with the rest of the media."

"Well, we'll just have to turn up the heat ourselves," Jamal said. "Let's recruit a bunch of students to call and email all the local media and ask them to cover the rally on Tuesday. If enough of us call they can't ignore us. Either way, we win—either with the publicity or an explanation that may put us one step closer to those responsible."

"I'll help," Gloria agreed, then hesitantly suggested they get together later to work on a phone tree.

"I'm sure you can handle it," Jamal said. "Just email everybody. I'll catch you later."

With that he abruptly walked away, leaving Gloria alone and embarrassed.

## CHAPTER TEN

Monday brought a whole new set of problems. Just as Gloria was leaving for class, the phone rang.

"Why don't you tell that loudmouth Jamal to just drop this whole thing?" said a female voice on the other end. "Tell him you believe this was just a prank and that you want to forget it. He'll listen to you. If he keeps on with these demonstrations, he's going to get himself hurt. Tell him that."

"Who is this?" Gloria demanded, dropping her books.

"Just let it go! Be glad no one's been hurt—yet," the caller said.

"Are you threatening us?" Gloria asked angrily, but the caller hung up.

***

At noon, Jamal found Gloria and Ashante in the Union, and his face was ablaze with rage.

"Have you seen this?" he asked furiously, thrusting a sheet of paper in front of them.

"What is it?" Ashante asked, as Gloria started to read it.

"A letter from the Dean," Jamal said. "He's asking each student organization to sign it."

"What does it say?" Ashante asked Gloria. "*We, the undersigned, support the administration's investigation into the cross burning incident and agree to cease participating in any rallies or demonstrations until the investigation is complete,*" Gloria read.

"Can you believe that?" Jamal said, grabbing the letter back from Gloria and crumpling it into a ball. "From what I hear, the Dean met with the head of each organization individually, except ours of course. The white frats have already signed, as have the

Young Republicans. That's all I've heard of so far, but I'm sure he'll get them all to sign it before he's through."

"He can't get away with this!" Gloria said.

"He can and he will," Jamal retorted. "Damn it! They're knocking our legs out from underneath us. We need the support of as many of the student organizations we can get. Without them, we're just a handful of blacks making noise—something they'll find very easy to ignore."

"Maybe it won't be that bad," Ashante said. "Look, there's Bruce. Let's see what he thinks."

"Hey, Bruce!" Gloria said.

"What's up?" Bruce asked.

"Have you seen the Dean's letter?" Jamal asked.

"Yeah, as a matter of fact, I just met with him," Bruce said, looking uncomfortable.

"And?"

"And I signed it," Bruce said, setting his jaw in a resigned expression bracing for Jamal's anger.

"You what?" Gloria asked, her voice rising.

"You heard him," Jamal said. "He sold us out!"

"Now, wait a minute! That's not fair," Bruce said.

"But why?" Ashante asked. "Why would you sign it?"

"Because this way the administration—,"

Jamal cut him off. "You back-stabbing coward! I don't know why I expected anything else."

"Hey, man," Bruce said, putting his hand on Jamal's arm.

"Don't touch me," Jamal said, shoving Bruce's hand away. "You sold us out. I've heard all I need to hear. Get out of my face."

Bruce raised his hands and backed away. "I'd really like to discuss this with you, man, but obviously you aren't in the mood. Maybe when you cool down, we can rap."

"You have nothing to say that I want to hear," Jamal said.

"I think you should leave now," Ashante said.

Bruce hesitated and then walked away.

"Well, that's it, then," Jamal said. "If the student body president signed, they all will. The administration has us right where they want us."

Jamal fought to regain his composure, while Gloria told him about the phone call she had received that morning warning them off.

"Did you call the police?" Jamal asked, and then laughed bitterly. "That's a stupid question. Like they'd care. Listen, do you think it's a good idea for the two of you to stay at your place alone?"

"We already talked that over," Ashante said, "and we're staying. We can't let them scare us off."

"Besides, whoever did this was obviously a coward," Gloria said. "I doubt if they'd try any physical violence. And we've got Rodriguez patrolling the place. We'll be all right."

"Well if you run into trouble, call me or Kwame, okay? We can be there in no time."

## CHAPTER ELEVEN

The administration's influence was felt at Tuesday's rally with less than thirty students showing up. Of those, only a handful— Donna Sullivan's group—were white.

A reporter approached Jamal. "I'm Steve Walsh from *The Herald*. Someone said you're in charge. Is that right?"

Jamal gave a curt nod. "Yeah, that's right."

"Well, what's the deal? I got a bunch of phone messages and emails saying this was going to be a massive demonstration. This is what you call huge?" He waved his hand at the small gathering. "I'll bet there's better attendance at Lakeside's intramural games."

"We were undermined by the administration," Jamal said. "And you can quote me on that."

"What do you mean?" Steve asked, whipping out his tape recorder.

"Dean Severson and President Horning coerced the other student organizations into signing an agreement to not participate in these rallies. You know—the old divide and conquer trick."

"Is that verifiable?"

"I'm sure you could get your hands on a copy of the agreement. Anyway I don't know what you're complaining about. You had a big story to run the other night when that cross burned, but you dropped the ball."

"Hey, I just write the stories. I don't get a say in whether they run or not," Steve said. "Although, I admit, that story did get chopped more than most."

"Who decided that?" Jamal asked.

"My editor, but it's strange, because usually that's the sort of story he tells me to run with."

"Who'd have that kind of pull?" Jamal asked.

Steve shrugged. "The owners. The big advertisers, maybe. I'll nose around a little. If I find out anything, I'll let you know. How's that?"

"What's in this for you?" Jamal said, remaining skeptical about this offer of help.

"Just say I'm helping out a friend. Now, how 'bout you get this rally going so it won't look like I was slacking off all afternoon?"

A few minutes later, Jamal stood before the small crowd. "As you can see, our numbers have dwindled significantly," he said. "And you will note, with the exception of our friends from White Students Against Racism, most of our other white allies have cut and run. It looks like we're on our own. The Dean has convinced most students that there is an official investigation going on behind the scenes. We know that is a smokescreen. I believe Severson and Horning think that if they can stall long enough, we will forget all about this. Well, they're wrong. If nothing else, they've made us more determined than ever to see this through. Only now it's an even tougher road ahead. Bruce signed the Dean's letter agreeing not to demonstrate. Without his support and resources, we have a major challenge in getting our views heard by the college authorities. But, hey, nobody said it was going to be easy, right?"

"Right!" The students replied in unison.

"Gloria and Ashante were targeted for this hate crime because they were black—plain and simple—yet the administration chooses to turn a blind eye. We cannot expect any help from them unless we can put them in a position where they have no choice but to respond to the truth. I don't know if that's possible. But, in the meantime, we can make things really uncomfortable on this campus, don't you think?"

The students roared, waving their fists in the air and barking their approval. Jamal led them in a chant: "No justice, no peace! No justice, no peace!"

The rally ended on a high note, but Jamal couldn't shake the feeling that he was fighting an uphill battle in taking on the administration. Despite his concerns, he knew deep in his heart that he would never waste a single moment on the thought of giving up.

That night he stirred until dawn, searching for a way to shake things up. He thought about an old Bible lesson his father used many times: *"when you get to the end of the road, remember, God is there."* The ideas began to flow.

Over breakfast, he outlined his plans to Kwame. "We'll hold a demonstration at the end of the month. It will be the biggest one this campus has ever seen."

"Sounds great, but how?" Kwame said. "I mean, with all the other student groups kissing the Dean's ass?"

"That's why I said at the end of the month," Jamal said. "That gives us a few weeks. By then, it should be obvious to everyone that Horning never launched, or had any intention of launching, an investigation. Hopefully we'll regain the students' support then. I'm going to contact the Black Student Organizations at the bigger campuses around the state and see if they'll each send a busload or two of their members to back us up. I'm counting on Steve Walsh to push hard for some decent coverage from *The Herald*. With this much time, we should have a hell of a turn out!"

"You know I'm with you, blood. I just want to know one thing," Kwame said.

"What's that?"

"Where do I have your remains shipped to, dog? Cause when this shit hits the fan, all hell is gonna break loose."

"Just make sure they take my shoes off," Jamal answered. "In the meantime, let's see what we can do about shaking things up around here."

***

The next day, BSO members gathered for a sit-in outside Horning's office. The president's secretary made a half-hearted attempt to get them to leave. When it became obvious the students weren't about to budge, she hastily retreated to the inner office.

Horning emerged and attempted to convince the students to leave. "This isn't helping your cause," he said.

"That's the root of the problem right there," Jamal said. "This shouldn't be viewed as our cause; it should be viewed as the University's cause."

"You're twisting my words," Horning replied. "Now, why don't all of you get back to class. You're here to get an education, which you're not going to get sitting cross-legged on my carpet. You've been informed that we're conducting an investigation. We're doing all that can be done at this time. Your presence here serves no purpose. You have the right to your views, but this is not the way to go about it. You people are actually hindering our efforts."

"Jail those responsible for this mess, and 'we people' will go away," Jamal retorted.

"At this point we have no evidence as to who the perpetrators are," Horning said.

"Well then, get used to us hanging around," Jamal said, folding his arms, "because we're going to be a very familiar sight. In fact, why don't we order in for lunch today?"

Horning stormed back into his office, muttering under his breath.

Elsewhere on campus, BSO protestors were having an effect. Black students bogged down the cafeteria service by holding up the lines, causing long delays. The black football players staged a sit-in during practice. Fliers were stapled up all over campus demanding action from the administration and condemning racial injustice.

Several classes had to be cancelled because students were making so much noise in the hallways, no one could hear the lectures. Parking became a nightmare when 100 standing signs declaring *No justice, No Peace* were placed all over the lots.

For over a week, the tension continued to build. Then, on a Monday morning, Jamal found a note in the BSO mailbox. "Back off, *monkey*," the note read, "or you'll have more than a cross burning to worry about." As he crushed the note, he heard loud laughter behind him. Five or six white guys were leaning against the wall across the way, snickering and staring at him.

"Which one of you sent this note?" Jamal said.

"What's the matter, militant? Got yourself a new pen pal?" a voice called from the back of the group.

"Come on out, you chicken shit, and say what you gotta say to my face," Jamal shouted.

"Hey boy, why don't you back off before you get in over your head?" another voice sneered. Jamal searched for its source and noticed a thin, pasty-faced student with dark stringy hair and tinted shades.

"Who the hell are you?" Jamal asked. "Or do you just answer to 'cracker'?"

The guy with the tinted shades just laughed. "Back off, *monkey*!" he said.

"You tell him, Rush!" one of the others shouted.

Jamal's rage exploded. He slammed Rush up against the wall with a loud thud. Instantly, the rest of the group laid into Jamal. Someone punched him in the side, just as another landed a blow across his temple. Another kicked him across the knees, so that he crumpled to the floor.

Finally, two campus security guards waded into the brawl and grabbed Jamal. He was relieved when the blows stopped raining down on him, but before he could catch his breath, he was dragged down the hall and shoved roughly out onto the sidewalk.

"The next time we catch you picking a fight boy, we won't treat you so nicely," one of the guards said, through gritted teeth.

"I didn't start anything. They're the ones who were harassing me!" Jamal protested. "They sent me a death threat and I'm sure they're the ones who have been calling my apartment inviting me to a 'sheet party'."

"We've heard all about you, Mr. Washington, and I'm sure anything you're getting isn't any worse than what you've been dishing out," the officer replied. "We heard you're planning some big demonstration. My advice to you is forget it. The administration's onto you, and if you don't learn to shut up, you just might get your black ass kicked off this campus!"

Before Jamal could reply, the security guards strode back into the Union, leaving him sputtering with rage. He rushed into the Dean's office, pushed past the secretary and confronted Severson.

"You see this?" Jamal shouted, pointing to his cut lip and his right eye that was rapidly swelling shut. "I'm getting threatening phone calls, death threats in the mail and now this! And to top it all off I just received some not-too-subtle threats from a couple of your campus pigs!"

Severson stood up from behind his desk. "Jamal, all of this can be avoided. Let's talk about it."

"I'm tired of talking. I want some action! Since you won't do anything, we will. Don't even think about trying to stop our demonstration, or I'll have the media, the NAACP and every other official body we can find screaming all over this place," Jamal said.

"Don't threaten me, Mr. Washington."

"Hey man, this isn't about a threat. This is about protecting black students."

With that Jamal stormed out of the Dean's office.

***

A few minutes later, Severson reported the entire incident to Horning.

"Your divide and conquer strategy is backfiring. We have to do something fast, or this university is going to explode!"

The phone rang. "Hold on Todd. Let me get this. This might be the call that will get us out of this damn mess," Horning said, as Severson paced the floor.

"What have you got for me?" Horning shouted into the receiver. He paused for a moment and listened. "It's worth a shot," he finally said. "Get in here and tell Severson. He'll be your point man."

Horning slammed down the phone. "Severson," he said, "you better pack your bags. It looks like you're going to Mississippi."

Severson stopped pacing. "What are you talking about?" he said.

"That was Ed Brown, the admissions guy. Apparently there's some sort of guru who lives in Mississippi and deals with this sort of thing. Brown's heard of him. He comes in, takes feuding students on retreats, and helps defuse situations like this, if you know what I mean. Ed said he was called in when they had the student riots at Central State last year and in three days he had calmed the tension on campus.

The door opened, and Ed Brown walked into the room. He glanced from Severson to Horning. "You filled him in?" he said.

Horning nodded. "You two get to work on this and convince him to get the hell up here. Be quick about it."

"What if he says no?" Severson asked.

"Don't give him a choice! Tell him we're drowning here! It'll be easier to convince him face to face. Get on the horn and find out where he is. Todd I want you on the next plane, train, or whatever the hell it takes. Got it?"

"I'll do my best," Severson sighed.

"You'll do more than that. You'll get it done! Do whatever is necessary to get him here, understood? This retreat thing might be the answer to getting us out of this damn crisis."

## CHAPTER TWELVE

About 800 miles away, Dr. Wendell Oliver reclined in his favorite chair and tried to relax. The fire crackled in the fireplace, casting dancing shadows on the cabin wall. Dr. Oliver was a tall man in his late 50s, with graying temples highlighting his deep-set eyes. He had aged well thanks to his daily walks with Queenie, his old blue-tick hound.

The smoky aroma of burning pine added to the soothing warmth of the flames. Soft jazz played in the background. Queenie nudged his arm gently. Dr. Oliver stroked her silky ears and smiled, as she sighed and rested her weight against his leg.

"That's a good girl," he said.

The cabin was his favorite place to be, deep in the Mississippi backwoods. He poured every ounce of his strength into the retreats, into helping students pursue the truth, and it left him feeling drained. After each retreat, this cabin, these woods, were his lush and soothing refuge.

Since his wife's death two years ago, he had come to the cabin more and more. Sarah had loved the cabin, too.

"I miss her, Queenie," Oliver said, looking at Sarah's picture on the fireplace mantle. Queenie responded with a thump of her tail.

"You miss her too, don't you, girl? Hard to believe it's been two years since she's been gone. We were one hell of a team."

Sarah had run their consulting business, talking with new clients, and taking care of all the arrangements. This had allowed him to concentrate on facilitating the retreats. Things had been slow at first. His friends had thought he was crazy to leave a tenured job at a prestigious university to strike out on his own.

"Sarah believed in my dream," he murmured to Queenie. "She knew what it's like to have a passion yearning to be set free. I couldn't have done it without her."

As Dr. Oliver looked around the room, his eyes were drawn to the large sliding doors that overlooked the lake. With Sarah hand in hand, they had spent many hours enjoying the view, watching the sunset, and wandering the trails along the lakeshore in peaceful seclusion.

Now a simple headstone marked Sarah's final resting place, nestled among the trees near the lake. Sarah had always called it the most beautiful place on earth, so he found it fitting that she rested there. His daily walks with Queenie always included a visit to the grave. It gave him comfort to know Sarah was at peace after her long, difficult battle with breast cancer.

It had been Sarah's idea to outfit the cabin with high-tech equipment to handle the demands of the business. He had been reluctant to give up complete escape from the world but had finally conceded that it was necessary. Sarah had even installed a phone system that automatically recorded all outgoing and incoming calls, freeing him from tedious note taking.

Since her death, he had limited his consulting to only a handful of contracts each year. This was difficult, because word-of-mouth now placed him in high demand. But without Sarah's support, he found it hard to rebound emotionally after each retreat. The country's racial woes weighed heavier on him with each passing year.

"Sometimes it's hard to see if I'm making a difference, you know that, Queenie?"

Dr. Oliver lit his pipe, drawing the sweet aroma into his mouth. He gently nudged Queenie aside and rose, gazing out at the lake and puffing silently. The late morning sun glistened through the trees that lined the path from the cabin to the shore. Queenie bumped against his leg. She whined and strained at a large red squirrel scampering between the trees.

"Leave him be, Queenie," he chided her. "That old squirrel has enough to do getting ready for winter. He doesn't need you harassing him. You wouldn't know what to do with him if you caught him, anyway."

Queenie returned to her rug by the fire and sank down with a sigh.

"Look at those leaves falling," Oliver murmured. "Autumn's here for certain, and winter's not far behind. Where has the time gone?"

It had been three months since his last retreat, yet he wasn't sure he was ready for another. During that retreat, a student had asked how he had become involved in race relations and why he had decided to devote his life to traveling across the country, trying to get whites and blacks to listen to each other. Dr. Oliver had brushed her off, saying somebody had to do it and he just happened to be that somebody. It was a trite answer, too pat and lacking in depth to have any real value. He felt guilty that he hadn't taken the time to give the student the answer she deserved. What he had failed to say required more time and pain than he had cared to spend, which led him to question his ability to continue as an effective leader.

"If I'm becoming too worn out to take the time to share my deepest beliefs and fears, how can I help others share theirs?" he asked aloud.

The lack of patience and rising skepticism was out of character for him. He had weathered many storms and helped many people successfully face theirs. He had grown up in the South in the 1950's when segregation was entrenched. Facing racism was a daily ordeal of survival.

Childhood memories played across his mind like old films. He remembered his parents' anger when a cross was burned on their street; beneath their anger had been a raw fear that had frightened him.

When he was nine, he bought an ice cream cone at a county fair. The ice cream vendor, a white man, had sneered and snickered. With his first lick, the ice cream tipped off the cone, and the biggest cockroach he had ever seen crawled out.

Oliver's experiences ranged from minor events, like white classmates openly being afraid to touch him, to the horrific—his older sister's rape by three white men. Vanessa had never been the same. He had always wondered if it would have made a difference if the rape had been reported to the police. At the time there had been too much fear. Who would believe the word of a 14-year-old black girl over that of white men?

He often retreated to books and found himself deeply moved by the writings of Dr. Martin Luther King Jr., Langston Hughes, and Mohandas Gandhi. Wendell would walk to school chanting Gandhi's mantra: "Be the change you want to see in the world." The more he chanted, the more he knew he couldn't just talk the talk, but had to live it. From that day forward, at age 12, his life's passion was found.

He became one of the first blacks to integrate the public schools in his hometown, despite the angry protests he faced. He integrated the minor league baseball team, persisting despite the taunts of "peanut butter" and worse from the opposing white players.

The positive memories of his upbringing were fewer, but they stood out. His first teacher at the new school had believed in him and showed him he had the ability to excel. He had never forgotten the kindness from this white teacher. Tom Parks, one of his white basketball teammates in junior high, had bought a bottle of pop one day and offered him a drink right out of the bottle. He was still amazed by the power of that simple gesture. "There is hope," he said out loud. "In the smallest gesture, there is hope."

The whirring of the fax machine interrupted his reverie.

*"We have a serious problem on our campus,"* the message read. *"A recent cross burning on the lawn of two LU students has led to an escalation of racial tensions, suspicions, and mistrust, polarizing the*

*campus. A series of protests, sit-ins and other disruptions have already taken place. In an effort to head off a major confrontation, and to return civility to our student body, we are in desperate need of your expertise. I have booked the first flight out to meet with you this evening. After you receive this fax, would you please call to confirm this meeting?"*

The message was signed, "Todd Severson, Dean of Students, Lakeside University."

Oliver paced the floor for nearly an hour, trying to decide if he should return the call. His soul felt exhausted and he wondered if he could muster the energy to intervene effectively. He finally turned to Queenie and found his answer.

Oliver called and explained to Severson that he only met with prospective clients on Wednesdays. "Also, I will need to speak to one of the student victims," he told the Dean.

"Is there any way your schedule can accommodate me today?" Severson asked. "I already have a flight reserved. And as far as talking with a student, I am perfectly capable of explaining the circumstances to you."

Dr. Oliver firmly repeated his conditions. "Now, are you still interested in my services?"

He heard Severson sigh into the phone. "Okay," Severson finally said, and started to ramble on about how eager he was to meet Oliver on Wednesday.

Dr. Oliver cut the conversation short. His initial reaction was one of distaste, but he would reserve final judgment for the face-to-face meeting just two days away.

He hung up the phone and turned to the dog. "We'll see what you think, Queenie."

## CHAPTER THIRTEEN

Wednesday morning found Gloria quivering on the steps of the Union, waiting to ride with Severson to the airport.

"I don't know how I got talked into this," she mumbled, her teeth chattering as much from nervousness as from the early morning chill. When Severson called her Monday afternoon, Gloria had hemmed and hawed. "This Dr. Oliver," she'd asked Severson, "what will he be doing, exactly?" Severson had explained that Oliver was a facilitator of sorts, that if they were lucky, he'd agree to lead the students on a retreat, where they could settle the brewing conflict once and for all. "You want that, too, don't you?" Severson had asked. Realizing it might be her only chance to force the administration to act, Gloria reluctantly agreed.

But Jamal had reacted with outrage over the idea. "They're stalling, that's all," he had warned. "They're trying to undermine our efforts to organize and shift everyone's attention to some brotherly love pow-wow in the woods!"

His words were echoing in Gloria's mind when Severson's car pulled up. The conversation on the ride to the airport was strained chitchat about the weather and the football team.

As soon as they were seated on the plane Severson ordered a Scotch on the rocks. He downed it in three gulps and hurriedly ordered another, explaining that he needed to settle his nerves before take-off. Gloria buried her face in a book of Maya Angelou poems, hoping to ward off any further conversation. After another drink, however, Severson got talkative.

"I think this retreat will be just what the doctor ordered, don't you?" he said.

Gloria frowned. "I think I need to learn more about it before I decide."

"Everything's going to be fine," the Dean said, patting her arm.

Gloria flinched at his touch and superficial assurances.

"These retreats are really effective, you know," he said. "I'm sure once we get everyone talking, things will work out."

"The only way this will be resolved is when justice is served," Gloria said, putting her book aside.

Severson scowled. "What do you mean by justice?"

"Catching and punishing whoever did this."

"We want the same thing, Gloria, but there is no evidence those two were involved," Severson said, waving to the flight attendant for a refill.

Gloria felt the goose bumps move down her back. She started to ask "which two," but she bit her lip. *Don't blow this*, she told herself sternly.

Instead, she bluffed, fishing for details. "Well, it sure looks like they had something to do with it," she said.

"What do you mean? Do you know something I don't?" Severson asked, apparently unaware of his blunder.

"Well, we're not sure if their voices are on the tape or not."

"I thought you lost the tape," he said, his voice surprised.

*Gotcha*, Gloria thought. As far as she knew, neither she nor Ashante had told Severson the tape was missing. "Fortunately, Ashante made a back up before that," she lied.

"A back up? Who else knows about this?"

"Just Ashante and me."

"You should have handed that tape over. I told you it was evidence!"

Gloria, realizing she wasn't getting anywhere by weaving a spider's web, changed the subject. "Why did you suppress my article—the real reason?"

"It ruffled too many feathers," Severson slurred, still under the effects of the scotch.

"Whose feathers?" Gloria asked.

"Never mind. You wouldn't understand. We're investigating; that's all that matters." Severson abruptly turned away, closed his eyes, and slipped into an alcohol-induced sleep.

The rest of the flight was uneventful, although Gloria kept mulling over their disturbing conversation. She took satisfaction in knowing she had planted some seeds of doubt in Severson's mind about the back-up tape. *Too bad we didn't really make a copy*, Gloria thought, as the plane landed.

Half an hour later, Severson was guiding the rental car through the Mississippi countryside, and Gloria was relieved to see the effects of the alcohol had worn off. The deeper into the woods they drove, the more breathtaking the landscape became. Thick foliage lined the roadside, and the sun poked its way through the leafy boughs arching overhead.

The leaves had almost all turned, and they showered the road in a spectrum of autumn colors. Listening to the crunch of the leaves beneath the tires, Gloria thought how much more pleasant this trip would be if Jamal was with her. Before she could dwell on that any further, the car rolled to a stop in front of a rustic cabin.

Dr. Oliver greeted them at the door and invited them inside, as Queenie inspected them.

"Hey there, old girl!" Severson said, reaching to pat her, but Queenie stiffened at his touch and moved out of his reach. Instead, the dog trotted over to Gloria and sniffed her pant leg with interest. She wagged her tail as Gloria reached down to gently stroke the dog's head. Gloria looked up and saw Dr. Oliver watching them. He gave a knowing smile and nodded. "Looks like she likes you," he said.

They moved into the living room, where Oliver offered them some lemonade and quickly got down to business. "What can I do for you?" he asked the Dean.

"Well, as I said in the fax, we have a bit of a problem on our campus," Severson began.

Gloria bit her lip several times to keep from interrupting as the Dean omitted details and added others to downplay the severity of the cross burning while laying the blame for most of the campus tension on the black student body. Several times during the Dean's account, Queenie paced between Oliver and Gloria but made no attempt to go near Severson.

"So, anyway, that's about it. We suspect this was just a very unfortunate prank, but now we have a handful of students accusing us of racism," the Dean concluded. "We need to get everyone together to talk this over so we can get on with the school year. I was told you're the best at leading this type of thing so here I am."

When the Dean finished, the room fell silent. In the awkward lull that followed, Severson reached out to pat Queenie, but she growled. When the Dean ignored this warning, Queenie wrinkled her muzzle in a snarl.

"I don't think your dog likes me," Severson said.

Dr. Oliver shrugged and patted the side of his chair. Queenie moved to lie beside him and fell silent. "I think she may need some fresh air. If you don't mind, Todd, I think I'll take Queenie outside. Gloria, would you join me?"

Gloria nodded, and as she stood up, Severson reached for the phone on the table beside his chair.

"Dr. Oliver," Severson said, "you don't mind if I use your phone to call my office, do you?" Severson asked. "My cell doesn't seem to get reception out here."

Dr. Oliver glanced at the recording equipment and smiled when he saw the green light that meant it was working. "Not at all," he said. "Help yourself."

***

As soon as the sliding door closed, Severson quickly dialed Horning's office.

"Well, is he willing to do it?" Horning asked impatiently.

"I'm working on it. But listen, there's something else. I may have let something slip on the plane ride down here."

"Like what?"

"Well, I may have mentioned something about two people being involved in the cross burning."

"What do you mean may have? What exactly did you say? Damn it, Todd! What were you thinking?"

"I had a few drinks. You know how I feel about flying. Anyway I didn't say which two. I don't think she even noticed. But that's not the main reason I'm calling. I thought the tape situation was handled. I told those two to get their hands on it and destroy it, but apparently the roommate made a copy."

"What?" Horning groaned. "I thought you were getting this under control, Todd. It sounds to me like its only getting worse!"

"I can't do anything about the tape from here. I thought maybe you could take care of that."

"Apparently, I'll have to," Horning replied. "You just make sure you get Oliver to agree to this. He's high profile enough to create some positive press, and we're going to need all of the spin we can get. I mean it. Do whatever it takes."

As they continued to plot strategy, Severson wished there was something stiffer to drink than lemonade.

## CHAPTER FOURTEEN

Gloria followed Dr. Oliver along the lakeshore path. It reminded her of the solitary walks she liked to take around the lake in Westport—*only this was far more peaceful*, she thought. Dr. Oliver strolled silently beside her, and Queenie ran ahead, sniffing the path and occasionally darting in between the trees.

Finally Dr. Oliver glanced down at her. "I'd like to hear your point of view," he said.

Gloria exhaled. She had told the story so many times, but always with a sense of fear and uncertainty. Here, with Dr. Oliver, she felt nervous but also safe. *As if this lake were some kind of salve*, she thought to herself.

In a quiet voice, she recounted the night of the cross burning. Only when she described the flames did her voice quiver. She told Oliver about the way the town police behaved, the newspaper article, the censorship, the stolen tape, the threatening phone calls, the smudged footprints, the conversation with Officer Rodriguez, and even the conversation she had with Severson on the plane.

"The Dean was right when he said we're angry," Gloria concluded. "He said they're taking action, but we've seen no evidence of it. They've undermined our efforts to organize, and they've turned the other student organizations against us. We want justice, pure and simple. We want our voices heard."

Dr. Oliver nodded, but he didn't say anything. They walked along a few more paces. Gloria realized he was waiting for her to continue.

"I don't know that much about this retreat business, but I'm willing to try anything. Lakeside is not a pleasant place to be anymore. It's costing a lot of money for my education, and I'm not getting one at this point."

"You make a good case," Oliver said. "Walk with me just a little further, please."

He took her to Sarah's grave and told her about Sarah and why her grave was there. He told her about the cross that was burned on his street when he was a child.

"Sarah and I started this work to help people in your very situation," Oliver said. "It's a struggle just to make it to college and an even greater one to succeed under the best of circumstances. When racism adds an even greater burden to that already heavy load, then something has to be done." He smiled at Gloria, but she saw something in his eyes that looked like sorrow. "I'd be happy to help you out," he told her. "I just need you to do something for me."

"What's that?" Gloria asked softly, moved by his concern and clear desire to help.

"Continue to let Severson think you have a back-up tape. Can you do that?"

"Sure, if you think it will help."

"Based on what you told me about your plane conversation and all that I've heard so far—."

"Dr. Oliver! Gloria!" It was Severson, hollering from a nearby grove of trees. "Where are you?"

"We're over here," Oliver called out, as the Dean stumbled through the woods to join them.

"We don't have much time left," Severson said. Gloria noticed small bits of twigs and leaves on the Dean's suit coat. "Our flight leaves in just a couple of hours. Have you reached a decision, Dr. Oliver?"

"I will facilitate your retreat," Oliver replied, holding out his hand to ward off Severson's obvious relief. "I do want to make one thing clear, however. I don't follow anyone else's agenda. There are no guarantees I'll get students to settle their differences. I've got to be free to take the discussion wherever it leads. After that, it's up to the students."

"Sure, sure, whatever," Severson said. "I just want this to happen quickly, before Jamal's so-called demonstration makes things worse."

"We can schedule it as soon as you'd like," Dr. Oliver said, "I'll fax you a complete agenda later in the week."

"I can't thank you enough," Severson said, as they made their way back to the cabin.

"Don't thank me yet," Oliver cautioned. "The hard part is still ahead." He stressed the importance of having all the student leaders at the retreat and any other students who had been outspoken during the crisis.

Severson headed to the car, but Gloria lagged behind for a moment.

"Talking with you has really been good for me," she said. "Thank you."

"You are the reason I do these retreats. You and others like you," Oliver said.

At that moment Sarah's presence was so great that he thought if he turned he would see her at his side. The tremors quickly passed, leaving him with a feeling of comfort and love. He always knew when he made the right decision because Sarah still found a way to show him.

He offered Gloria his hand, but she spontaneously hugged him.

"Thank you," she said, as Queenie bounded around them, baying cheerfully.

"Besides," Oliver said with a chuckle, "I could hardly turn you away when Queenie is so taken with you. She's an excellent judge of character."

"That would explain why she almost tore the Dean's pant leg off," Gloria said, as they shared a moment of warm laughter.

Oliver watched until the car drove out of sight along the winding drive. Despite his hesitation, he could already feel the surge of adrenaline that came with a new challenge.

"Here we go again, Queenie," he said giving the dog a playful thump on the ribs.

"You know, girl, my gut tells me there's something peculiar about this case. From everything that Gloria has told me, this may be about more than just racism."

## CHAPTER FIFTEEN

The weekend for the retreat quickly arrived, and the air on campus was swirling with excitement and trepidation. Gloria reached the crowd of students milling on the Union steps, hoping to find Ashante.

Diversions were abundant between a touch football game going, rap music blasting, and a swarm of neon orange Frisbees floating through the air.

Gloria saw Bruce and Donna Sullivan engrossed in an animated discussion. Chris Polaski, who had the unfortunate run in with Chuck Johnson the night of the cross burning, sat on the steps alone, reading.

*Where is she?* Gloria thought. When Gloria left the house, Ashante had still been in the bathroom fussing with her hair.

"The retreat will be over by the time you decide you're beautiful," Gloria had teased.

Ashante told Gloria to go ahead, saying she would join her at the bus stop. As the time neared for the retreat bus to arrive, Gloria worried whether her roommate would make it at all.

"There you are, G.W."

"It's about time," Gloria said, returning Ashante's contagious smile. "I was beginning to think you were a no-show!"

"We're a team, sis. Besides Tyrone, you're the only other person I would go on this retreat with. He's coming down next weekend. I can't wait. And speaking of men, there's Jamal!" Ashante suppressed a grin as Gloria's head whipped around.

Gloria's heart beat a little faster as she watched Jamal and Kwame approach. As they neared, she could hear their conversation.

"I'm telling you, Kwame, this is just another way for the administration to undercut our demonstration. They think if they can get us to roast a few hot dogs and sing songs around a campfire, all of this will just magically vanish. We've got to make sure we don't forget why we're here. Spending a weekend eating s'mores and spilling our guts about our 'cultural differences,' as they put it, won't change what's happened."

"If you're so sure this is a waste of time then why are you even going?" Kwame asked.

"Someone has to keep the heat on," Jamal said, as he pushed his way past Gloria and Ashante with barely a nod in their direction. "We can't let the administration think they're off the hook for their inaction just because they're picking up the tab for this cultural cook-out. Besides, all the student leaders, and maybe the crackers who burned that damn cross, will be there. I wouldn't miss a chance to confront them for anything in the world."

Gloria frowned and quickly felt Ashante's hand on her arm. "What's wrong, G.W.?" Ashante asked," why the worried look?"

"I just overheard Jamal. I hope he's wrong and this isn't just an attempt to whitewash the whole thing."

"We won't let that happen," Ashante said, squeezing Gloria's arm.

"I've had my head in the sand all these years," Gloria said softly. "I mean, I heard the horror stories, but it was always something that happened to other people. My eyes are open now. It's like for the first time I'm wide awake. You know what I mean?"

"You're starting to sound like Jamal," Ashante said with a smile. "I can't wait to hear you after a whole weekend with that man!"

"I have a feeling I'll be the last thing on Jamal's mind this weekend," Gloria said. "To him, I'm just a very small part of a very big cause. If that cross had burned in someone else's yard, he would never have even spoken to me. As it is, the only time we talk is when he needs me to speak at another rally. Don't get me wrong, I'm as eager as he is for justice."

"But?"

"But it might be nice if he didn't look right through me," Gloria admitted reluctantly.

"I knew it!" Ashante squealed. "You've got it bad!"

The roar of a sputtering engine drowned out their conversation, much to Gloria's relief. An old yellow school bus pulled up to the curb in front of the waiting students.

"Damn, that can't be our ride!" someone groaned. Murmurs of discontent started to build into a loud hum. The grumbling didn't last long, however, as the school bus pulled further ahead and a full cruise Charter took its place at the curb. There was a collective sigh of relief. The students pushed forward to the bus and stashed their gear in the wide, ample storage area.

Carolyn Ford, Lakeside's director of student activities, was in charge of the bus boarding. "Before you board, take one of these index cards and put one of these colored stickers on your jacket where it can easily be seen," she told the group. "You are to sit with a person who has the same color of sticker as you have."

Rush Haughman and his Sigma brother, Stu Barton, were standing a few feet in front of Gloria and Ashante.

"Social engineering. That's all we need," Rush muttered loudly. "I hate this stupid trip already."

"Hey, look at it this way," Stu said. "So we're stuck in the woods for a couple of days. All we have to do is make it through this and then things can get back to normal around here. We won't have to listen to any more whining about racism and all that black bullshit."

Gloria glared at the back of Stu's head, then glanced at Ashante and rolled her eyes, as the line of students began to move.

\*\*\*

The bus boarding continued at a slow pace as students found their assigned seats. Ashante was paired with Dan Trent, a white student she hadn't met before. Dan was fairly tall with sandy brown hair parted on the side, his face framed by oversize glasses.

Ashante had heard through the grapevine that he was a member of the Sigma fraternity on campus along with Rush and Stu. She expected him to object to sitting with her, but he appeared more nervous than anything. He barely returned her greeting, and they lapsed into an uncomfortable silence.

Gloria looked around, but she didn't see anyone with a sticker that matched hers, so she sank into an empty seat, feeling conspicuous. A moment later Donna Sullivan slid into the seat with her.

"Hi!" Donna greeted her in a cheerful voice. "How've you been?"

Gloria smiled. "Busy."

"Yeah, things have been crazy. The Dean's all bent out of shape because I wouldn't sign his letter."

"You didn't sign it?"

"No, way. I didn't see any action coming from the administration. Speaking of Dean Severson, I heard you took a trip with that creep. How'd that go?"

"About like you'd expect. It was worth it, though, to get this retreat together."

"This had better work out," Donna said. "Otherwise we're joining the Black Student Organization in confronting the administration. We'll take it to the press, the trustees, the alumni, whatever it takes!"

"Donna, I don't know if anyone's said this yet, but I want to thank you for all of your support. You've really been there from the beginning."

"That means a lot, Gloria. We want our organization to be known as one BSO can count on."

Three rows ahead, Stu sat with Chuck Johnson. Stu's pained expression said it all, as he stared at the index card he had been given. The directions at the top read: "Ask your seatmate the following questions. When was your first encounter with a person of a different race?" *When we kicked that nigger's ass, the one who got lost and wandered onto our block*, Stu thought.

Next question: "Was it a positive experience?" *Well, he positively got his ass kicked*, Stu smirked.

He had grown up in an all-white neighborhood. Any black person who wandered into their neighborhood without a good reason had been automatically subjected to an ass kicking. That's just how it was.

Stu realized in a few moments he would have to find a way to recount this experience to Chuck. He also realized the odds of him being able to do so without getting punched were slim to none. The smirk faded.

"We are about to get underway," Ms. Ford announced. "I want to welcome all of you to this retreat. For those of you who were formally invited, you were selected as ideal candidates for this trip. For the rest of you who volunteered to attend, we appreciate your interest and presume your reasons for attending are appropriate.

"As you know, Lakeside is facing some difficult challenges. The purpose of this trip is to engage in constructive dialogue and to find a way to meet those challenges. So let's get started. Look at the index card you received when boarding. Use those questions to interview your seatmate. You will introduce your seatmate to the group later this evening. Remember, the purpose of this is to get to know each other better."

The bus headed out of the city and soon filled with steady chatter as the students started their interviews.

"Why did you sign up for this retreat?" Gloria asked Donna, reading from the index card.

"Well, you know, I'm the president of White Students Against Racism. This is the type of thing we want to get involved in," Donna answered, distractedly, her eyes wandering through the bus. Her eyes lingered on a couple of the black guys. She wasn't about to tell Gloria that they were the other reason she was here. Donna felt a shiver of excitement trace its way down her spine.

Gloria cleared her throat. "Donna?"

"Sorry," Donna said, reluctantly leaving her daydream. "What were you asking?"

Near the front of the bus, Ashante was getting frustrated. Dan limited his answers to one or two words. He stared at his hands, which he kept clenched in tight fists in his lap. When it was Dan's turn to interview Ashante, he asked the questions so quietly she had to lean in close to hear him.

"I'm on the retreat because the cross was burned in my yard," she told him.

"Are you all right with it? I mean, does it still bother you?" Dan asked, avoiding her gaze.

*That question wasn't on the card*, Ashante thought. She wanted to reply, "Are you for real," but she held back. "Absolutely it still bothers me. I still get scared sometimes at night and I know it will take me a long time to get over it. It will help a lot when the people who did it finally get caught."

Dan looked directly at her for the first time. "Do you know who did it?" he asked.

"No, but we're working on it. And if I'm losing sleep, I know its affecting Gloria ten times as much as me."

"How's that?"

"She was really naive when it came to things like this. She always expected the best of everybody. Now she has nightmares all the time."

"I never thought about it getting to her so much."

"Why would you think about it at all?"

"Well, I didn't—I mean—never mind," Dan muttered, dropping his glance again.

Meanwhile, Jamal found himself at a loss for words for one of the few times in his life. His seatmate was Mark Serra, president of the Ten Percent Club, Lakeside's gay student organization. Mark wanted to skip the interviews and spend the time explaining to Jamal how much blacks and gays had in common.

Jamal couldn't believe his string of bad luck. It was hard enough to sit with a white guy for the entire two-hour bus ride, but a gay guy, too? Jamal wondered which one of the trip coordinators was getting a private chuckle over their seating assignment.

Jamal's irritation grew as Mark continued to describe how much they had in common. In Jamal's opinion, gays were riding the coattails of the black civil rights movement. *It's different*, he thought, trying to figure out a way to change seats. *After all, gays don't have to wear their group association on their sleeves, but we can't escape our skin color.*

A disturbance near the front of the bus drew everyone's attention. Chuck and Stu were engaged in a heated argument, their voices rising.

"Listen, wise ass," Chuck said, "either you stop with the snide comments, or I'll fix it so you can't comment on anything, you dig?"

"Lighten up homey," Stu retorted, his face flushed bright red and the muscles near his temples twitching noticeably. "All I said was I dislike coons. You know those masked, furry little animals with the ringed tails?"

"That's not what you meant, and you know it!" Chuck yelled.

"What else would I have meant?" Stu asked, feigning innocence. "Haven't you ever seen a coon? Or are possums all they grow down there in Alabamy?"

Chuck's fist connected a glancing blow to Stu's mouth. Stu swung at Chuck's nose. Jamal leaped from his seat and joined Professor Reese and Professor Taylor, two of the faculty members accompanying the group, in separating the two. Jamal quickly pulled Chuck away.

"Let go of me, man. I'm going to knock his teeth in," Chuck shouted, lunging toward Stu.

"This ain't the place, brother!" Jamal said, continuing to hold Chuck back.

Stu silently wiped the blood from the corner of his mouth and returned to his seat, obviously subdued by a comment from Professor Reese.

Jamal turned to his seatmate. "Hey, Mark," he said. "You mind swapping seats with my buddy, Chuck?"

The rising tension on the bus felt explosive, as if the windows would blow out at any moment. Mark got up and switched seats with Chuck.

Ms. Ford got back on the intercom: "We all must show some restraint," she said. "You are all adults, and it's time you begin to act like it."

"Yeah, can't we all just get along?" a voice drawled from the back of the bus.

Bruce stood up in his seat in the center of the bus. "Everybody, tone it down," he said. "Or else this is going to be a long weekend."

"Everything's under control," Ms. Ford continued. "Let's get back to the interviews. When you are finished with those, you have one other assignment. Each of you is to demonstrate something from your culture that involves touching, such as a way of styling hair, or a handshake, or a hand game."

"How 'bout a hand job?" another voice called from the back of the bus invoking laughter and breaking the tension.

Ms. Ford ignored the outburst. "The reason for this exercise," she explained, anticipating their questions, "is that many people, including some of you here, have never physically touched someone who is racially different. The mere act of touching may help you overcome some of your misconceptions."

"Stu just got touched!" Kwame yelled, setting off a ripple of laughter. "How was it, Stu?"

Jamal was glad he was sitting with Chuck and didn't have to participate in the exercise. Stu pretended to nap in the seat, rather than talk to Mark. *First a nigger, now a fag*, he thought.

Many of the students quickly shook hands just to get the exercise over with. By the time the bus rolled into the campsite, most had switched seats to sit with their friends. When the bus doors opened, the students poured out, eager to get up and stretch cramped muscles and escape the unspoken tension that had seemed to grow over the course of the bus ride. The students clumped together with their friends, waiting for their bags, and looked around uneasily. A single question was on most of their minds: *How in the hell is this weekend going to turn out?*

## CHAPTER SIXTEEN

At the retreat site, each student was paired with a roommate of a different race. Gloria was happy to be rooming with Lori Christianson—at least they had the *Campus Tempo* in common. Ashante roomed with Judith Hall, a white sorority sister whom she knew from life in the dorm. Jamal was relieved to be bunking with a football player who at least appeared to be straight.

As soon as the students settled into their rooms, an announcement directed them to meet at the campsite's Great Hall. Jamal, Kwame and Chuck joined Gloria and Ashante on the walk to the meeting. The other black students joined them, and by the time everyone entered the Great Hall, the forty students in attendance had become two distinct groups, divided by race. The two groups found seats in the meeting room, maintaining their distance from each other.

After getting the students' attention, Ms. Ford said a few words of welcome and then introduced Dr. Oliver. The room quickly filled with whispers as he strode from the back of the hall to the podium.

He looked around the room, and when he saw Gloria, he gave an almost imperceptible nod. "Everything we do this weekend will have a meaning and a message," Dr. Oliver began, his voice carrying easily through the hall. "Now, I understand you're having a bit of a problem on your campus."

The students broke into nervous laughter.

"In light of this," Dr. Oliver continued, "I want to make one point clear from the start. This weekend has been designed to explore race relations. In order for this to be successful, however, we must allow ourselves to focus on the things we have in common as fellow human beings. Too often we attempt to relate to each other solely from the rigid racial categories we have created."

Oliver left the podium and walked toward the students. As he reached the group of white students, he extended his hand to a young woman in the front row and pulled her to her feet.

"What's your name?" he asked her.

"Marjorie Phillips," she said.

"Well, Marjorie, I am Wendell Oliver, and by the time this weekend is over, I hope we will be friends. First of all, though, what race am I?"

"You're black—um, I mean, African American," Marjorie said.

"You're right!" Oliver said with a smile. "And you, my dear, are white, Caucasian, correct?"

Marjorie nodded, as several of the students chuckled.

Dr. Oliver frowned. He turned from Marjorie to face the group. "The laughter here tells me you all think this exchange is rather trivial," he said. "But the fact is, we needed to get that out of the way first. Now we can set the issue of skin color aside and get working on our friendship."

He motioned Marjorie back to her seat. "You see, if Marjorie and I are going to be friends, we have to interact as people, not as colors. If I try to relate to Marjorie solely as a black person, then it is going to be very difficult, because I'm going to be carrying with me all the baggage of my culture and race. Marjorie, in turn, will have to respond to me as a white person. With all that baggage, we'll have to meet outside, because there won't be any room big enough for us!"

More laughter greeted his words, and the tension in the room slowly began to ease.

"If we can interact simply as people first, then we can bring in our cultural differences later. We can use them to enhance the relationship, rather than having them act as roadblocks. That applies to each and every one of you, not just to Marjorie and me,"

Dr. Oliver smiled. "That concludes the first lecture. Fairly painless, right? Now, let's have some fun, shall we? First, let's get rid of these chairs and take a seat on the floor in one big circle, symbolizing the unity we hope to establish this weekend."

As the other students began clearing chairs, Jamal moved to the center of the room and caught Dr. Oliver's attention. "Sir, with all due respect," Jamal said, "this is all well and good, but we have some serious issues we need to address. I don't think we should waste time with fun and games." He pointed to Gloria and Ashante. "These sisters had a cross burned on their front lawn, and the cops and campus administrators are trying to cover it up. The BSO won't let that happen. We've led a number of campus demonstrations. We've tried to work with the white student organizations, but they've sold us out."

Several white students shouted their objections, but Jamal spoke over them.

"We're here to obtain some redress," he said. "We want some action, some justice. I'm not here to play games this weekend or to educate whitey."

"Thank you," Oliver said, "tell me, what is your name?"

"Jamal Washington."

"Jamal, you have raised legitimate concerns. Will you trust me to address those concerns in due time?"

After a lengthy hesitation, Jamal shrugged and gave a brief nod.

"I admire your passion for justice as you see it," Oliver said, "but, before there can be justice, there has to be dialogue—genuine communication. I can't know what someone wants until they tell me. Let me give you and your fellow students an example."

The chairs had been stacked along the walls, leaving a wide space in the middle of the room. Dr. Oliver directed the group to gather there and form three circles.

"Jamal, I will need your assistance," he said. "Have the students in each circle count off, from one, up to the number in their group. Make sure each person remembers his or her number. Now have them mix themselves up so that they are out of order, so that one is not next to two, four is not next to five, and so forth. The goal of this activity is for the circles to compete with each other, to be the first with all of its members back in the correct order."

The students followed the instructions and waited expectantly.

"There is a catch," Oliver said. "To get back in order you must close your eyes, and you cannot speak. If you open your eyes or talk, you eliminate your group. You can laugh, however. Jamal will watch to make sure you don't cheat! When you think your group is back in the correct numerical order, the entire group should clap hands. Okay, close your eyes. Ready, set, go!"

The students stumbled and groped around, and nervous laughter filled the room as they bumped into each other. When students in one circle started clapping their hands, Jamal verified they were in the correct order. The group erupted in cheers.

"How were you able to get back in the right order without talking or looking?" Oliver asked.

"I remembered where my original position in the circle was," said one student, and many nodded in agreement.

"What is the meaning of this activity?" Oliver asked. "Is it just about memory? What if your circle had fifty people in it? Could you remember where everyone's place was?"

Dr. Oliver explained the purpose of the activity was to show the importance of communication—without it, it's like trying to run in the dark. He pointed out how some people communicated their numbers through touching, holding up the right number of fingers, or stomping their feet the appropriate number of times.

"With communication we can put things back in order. Do you understand, Jamal?"

"We'll see," Jamal said.

"I think we're ready for some more in-depth introductions now, so we can get to know each other better," said Dr. Oliver. "Everyone take a seat on the floor, and we'll begin."

The students were instructed to introduce their seatmates from the bus, using the information they gathered from the index-card interviews. The person being introduced was asked to stand. Chuck was selected to start. He snarled as Stu lumbered to his feet and refused to look in Stu's direction.

"That's Stu Barton," Chuck said. "He's German. Um, he doesn't have a job right now, but he's hoping to land one with his dad's company when he graduates next year, so he's majoring in finance and business administration. I couldn't get a straight answer from him regarding why he came on this retreat. He made it sound like he didn't really have a choice. As far as his likes and dislikes, I'm not sure what he likes, but he obviously dislikes me!"

More nervous laughter greeted this comment. Stu started to respond angrily but glanced at Dr. Oliver and quickly dropped his eyes to the floor. He gave a stiff, yet fairly accurate introduction of Chuck, without indulging in any slurs.

The introductions continued, most of them limited to bare-bones detail, suggesting most of them hadn't taken the opportunity to really get to know each other or were afraid to be truthful.

When it was Jamal's turn, he found it difficult to conceal his discomfort. "Mark Serra is of Norwegian descent. He works with the Community Players Theatre Group in the city and hopes to get a fulltime position with the troupe when he graduates in May, with his degree in theatre arts." Jamal recited the facts as quickly as possible, avoiding the friendly smile Mark flashed his way. "Uh, he said he came on this retreat because he wants to work for equality for everyone. That's about it."

"Well, not quite," Mark said, remaining on his feet. "I'm also here as president of the Ten Percent Club. For those of you who aren't familiar with us, we're the campus organization for gays and lesbians. I'm here representin', dog," he joked.

Several students exchanged sideways glances. A dark-haired guy sitting next to Jamal nudged him with an elbow and whispered, "Bet you're glad he was just your seatmate, not your roommate, huh?"

"You said it," Jamal agreed, but he felt a twinge of guilt as he watched Mark bravely facing down the whispers and frowns that greeted his announcement.

"Not many students are familiar with our organization. Everyone thinks we just sit around with limp wrists and drink espresso," Mark said. "Well, that's why I'm here—to try to change those views. We're people. That's all. We're a minority, true, but we're still human beings. It's the same for us as for other minorities. We all just want respect."

"Great, just what we need—a weekend retreat in Granolaville, stuck out here with all the nuts, flakes, and now fruits!" Rush muttered, just loud enough to be heard by those near him.

Stu laughed. Kwame, who was close enough to overhear the two, leaned over and whispered in a harsh voice, "So, Rush, which category do you fit in?"

Before Rush could respond, Dr. Oliver noticed their exchange. "Something you fellas want to share with us?" he asked. They hastily shook their heads.

The introductions continued. Donna introduced Gloria as "one of the innocent victims on whose lawn that hideous cross was burned." She added that as the president of WSAR, she personally felt "the entire incident was appalling and reflected horribly on Lakeside as a whole."

Dan introduced Ashante. "This is Ashante Melashe. She's majoring in broadcasting, and she works at the Cable Access Channel part-time. She's here because she's Gloria's housemate and the cross was burned in her yard, too. She dislikes bigots and public speaking. She likes sports. All in all, she's just a nice ordinary person, it seems like."

"You sound surprised by that," Oliver said.

"Well I never really knew anyone like her before."

"Anyone black, you mean!" Jamal snapped.

"Easy, Jamal," Oliver cautioned him.

"It's just that Gloria and Ashante were just names before. Talking to Ashante on the bus made her more real, you know." Dan looked embarrassed. Rush and Stu glared at him as he quickly looked away.

It was Ashante's turn to introduce Dan, and she admitted she had been apprehensive about having him for a seatmate. "The fraternity guys he hangs around with aren't exactly known for friendliness toward black people, but Dan is actually quite decent. He's an engineering major and works as an assistant to the Buildings and Grounds supervisor on campus. He likes rock music and Steven Seagal movies. He dislikes no-win situations. I'm not sure what he means by that, but that's what he said."

Dan looked increasingly uncomfortable as Ashante continued; as soon as she finished, he quickly excused himself and hurried out of the room.

The rest of the introductions wrapped up without incident. "Now that we're warmed up," Oliver said, "we have one more exercise for those who lack photographic memories and need another go at everyone's name. Starting with you," he said, pointing at Marjorie, "and going clockwise, I want each of you to repeat your full name, then give us a one-word description of how you feel."

"Marjorie Phillips. Um, optimistic."

"Donna Sullivan. Hopeful."

"Bruce Saxton. In tune. Oops, that's two words. How about—happenin'."

The exercise proceeded around the circle, until it was Jamal's turn.

"Jamal Washington. Angry." Jamal looked at Kwame, who was seated next to him, and nodded.

"Kwame Brooks. Bitter."

"Pissed off," said a lanky basketball player, ignoring the one-word limit.

"Ashante Melashe. Hurt."

"Gloria Wilson. Victimized."

The tension flooded back into the room as several more students opened up and voiced their true feelings.

"Chris Polaski. Resentful."

"Lori Christianson. Disillusioned."

The tension increased further as Rush and his cronies took their turns.

"Rush Haughman. Scapegoat."

"Stu Barton. I feel like a walking target."

"You're supposed to use only one word, dumb ass," Chuck growled. "Or should I call you 'bull's-eye'?"

"Back off, boy," Stu shouted jumping to his feet.

"I'm not your boy," Chuck replied, standing, too. "You need me to prove that to you again, or was the ass kicking I gave you on the bus enough?"

Dr. Oliver cleared his throat. "It looks like we have our first volunteers for the Peace Tent," he said. "Right out that door, gentlemen, you will find a tent. You will both go inside and remain there until you can be civil to one another. You do not have to become best friends, but you do need to lose the attitudes and find a way to get along. Agreeing to disagree is fine, as long as you can do it in an acceptable manner. Professor Reese will accompany you."

Muttering and swearing under their breath, both Chuck and Stu followed Professor Reese from the room.

"The Peace Tent is not designed to be a punishment," Oliver told the group. "Rather it is intended to provide an opportunity for those in opposition to really listen to one another. The real goal is to respect each other's right to be heard and to have all viewpoints considered. Some of you will not have to go to the Peace Tent, although all are welcome. Others will find they spend more time there than anywhere else during this retreat."

Kwame nudged Jamal. "Hey, man! Hope you like the smell of canvas. You know your ass is going to be parked in that Peace Tent all weekend!"

Jamal smiled grimly. "It's going to take more than a pup tent and pretty words to distract me. I'm here to make sure we stay on task."

Dr. Oliver cleared his throat again. "I believe we're done with the warm-up exercise. We'll be getting to supper shortly. Let's do a quick review of the rules for this weekend. You'll find them listed in the handbook each of you will get on your way out. First, it's very important that you use the buddy system." Oliver's voice sharpened to a business-like tone. "There are no exceptions to this rule. Safety comes first, and that means not going it alone while we're out here. The second rule is, half of your free time must be spent with a person of a different race."

The students shifted uneasily and several looked clearly alarmed.

"Come on, people," Oliver said, his tone softening. "Most of the activities you enjoy doing with your friends you can enjoy doing with someone new. Play sports, go for a walk or, better yet, just use the time to talk and listen. You may be surprised to find out what you have in common."

Many students appeared unconvinced. Donna, however, found the idea quite intriguing. She hoped most of her cultural mingling would be with one of two guys she singled out as definitely having potential, Kwame or Chuck. Kwame's sense of humor and easy smile appealed to her, although with his hair in dreadlocks and a flashy earring, his look was a bit too Jamaican for her taste.

Chuck definitely had the lead in the looks department, she told herself, having noted the way his biceps and chest muscles stretched the material of his red T-shirt. He was well over six feet tall with a solid football player's frame. His hair was short and parted on the side. His dark skin and full lips led Donna to think all sorts of unexpected thoughts. She even found his fiery temper appealing and fully appreciated his irritation with Stu.

"I want to remind everyone of perhaps our most important rule," Oliver continued, "that whether you agree with someone's opinion or not, you need to debate the issues, not attack each other. Now, let's get to supper. Learning to get along is hungry work! I'm not sure what's on tonight's menu but tomorrow night we're in for a treat—a real soul food feast. Men have clean-up duty tonight, women tomorrow night, and everyone gets to pitch in on Sunday."

As the students got to their feet and gathered their things, Dr. Oliver added, "Don't forget to grab one of these handbooks. You'll want to look it over tonight to prepare for tomorrow. After supper, we'll take a quick tour of the campsite, and then we'll meet back here for a discussion session."

Gloria bumped into Jamal as they joined the group pressing toward the door. "You feel okay about it so far?" she asked.

Jamal grimaced. "If this is a sign of what's to come, I'd bet we head back to campus no better off than we are now."

## CHAPTER SEVENTEEN

Supper was subdued as most of the students were tired from the long bus ride and the strain of forced interaction. Yet Dr. Oliver was pleased to see at least some of them mingling, rather than sitting strictly divided by race. Gloria and Ashante joined Judith, Lori and Donna at a small table. Conversation was confined to talk of classes and professors, steering clear of any controversial topic.

Jamal's table quickly filled with brothers, eliminating any chance for someone new to break into his circle. As soon as everyone was seated, Jamal launched into another call for action.

"This is nothing but a feel-good distraction," he told them. "I overheard them talking about follow-up activities when we get back to Lakeside. I've got my follow up—the demonstration already in the works. We have to show the administration we see through their scheme. They're trying to look all sympathetic and concerned by sponsoring this retreat, but I'm not buying it."

As his tablemates dug into their full plates, Jamal left his untouched. "Lakeside is a breeding ground for discrimination against our people," he continued. "It has to be stopped, as brother Malcolm would say: 'by any means necessary'. A weekend in the woods is not going to do the trick. We need a united front to show we're not going to take this anymore. The demonstration will do just that. We'll make sure the administration has to sit up and take notice."

Suddenly Jamal felt someone tapping him lightly on the shoulder. He looked up to see Gloria standing next to their table.

"Sorry to cut in," she said, "but Dr. Oliver asked me to help lead the discussion tonight, and I wondered if you wanted to say a few words. Nothing major, just something to get the discussion rolling."

"Tight," Jamal replied, "although I'm not sure they'll like what I have to say. I'm not in the mood to take any bull from anyone."

"I guess we'll find out what happens when the featured speaker has to leave halfway through his speech to sit in the Peace Tent!" Kwame said teasingly.

Jamal flipped Kwame the finger as the others at the table burst into laughter. Gloria continued to stand at Jamal's side, feeling awkward, until he noticed that she was still there.

"What time is the meeting?" he asked.

"Seven-thirty."

"Right, see you then, Gloria," Jamal said, turning back to his friends.

"G.W.," Gloria said.

"What?" Jamal asked, looking over his shoulder at her.

"Well, it's just that most of my friends call me 'G.W.,' and since we spend so much time together working on this thing, I thought..."

"Sure, whatever," he said vaguely, returning to his conversation.

Gloria's face flushed hot and she quickly walked away. *Stupid, stupid, stupid*, she chastised herself as she made her way back to her table. *Jamal doesn't even know I exist; much less consider me his friend. I'm just part of the cause, nothing more.*

"Real smooth," Kwame chided Jamal.

"Yeah, way to blow it, player," Chuck joined in.

Jamal looked at them, bewildered. "What?" he said.

"Just tell me this—what's wrong with you?" Kwame asked.

"With who?" Jamal's mind was already back on the demonstration.

"With you, dog. I mean, why are you dissing a fine sister like that? She's obviously interested and you act like you don't even see her!"

"Word—I got to agree with my man here," Chuck said. "You shut her down cold, and in my opinion, that's one classy lady. She deserves better than that."

"So what gives?" Kwame asked. "You got something better lined up that you can't give her the time of day?"

"I don't know what you're talking about," Jamal said. "She's not interested in me. She wanted me to speak at the meeting tonight, that's all."

"Man, if you can't tell that woman's interested, then maybe you better hook back up with your buddy Mark," Chuck said, earning the finger again. "Those puppy eyes she gave you ain't got nothin' to do with no meeting, except maybe one she's hoping for later tonight in a less crowded place."

"We're telling you, Little Malcolm, that girl's down for you. You got to be blind not to see it," Kwame said. "Your game is slipping, brother!"

"I don't have time for this bullshit," Jamal said, pushing back his chair. "I'll catch you guys later."

"Don't forget we got kitchen duty. Speaking of women on the make and guys too dumb to notice," Kwame said, zeroing in on Chuck. "What's the deal with that Donna chick?"

"Who's Donna?" Chuck asked, taking his turn at looking confused.

"Donna Sullivan," Kwame said. "The blonde with the sexy build, president of the White Students Against Prejudice, or whatever they call it. You know, that bunch of white do-gooders always running around campus acting like they're our best friends."

"So, what are you saying?" Chuck asked.

"She's been eyeballin' you all evening, dog." The other guys at the table nodded.

"Get outta here!" Chuck rolled his eyes in disbelief.

"I'm telling you, man, it's your big chance to make a booty call."

Chuck turned and scanned the dining hall. He spotted Donna leaving with Gloria. Their eyes met and Chuck flashed her a wide smile, testing Kwame's theory. Donna's face flushed scarlet as she returned his smile, looking back over her shoulder at him as she left the dining hall.

"All, right!" Kwame exclaimed, reaching over to bang fists with Chuck. "It's your play, bro!"

Chuck answered with a wide grin.

After supper the guys headed into the kitchen for dish duty. Jamal reappeared, but was uncharacteristically quiet. As he grabbed a rag to dry some dishes, he overheard Rush whining to Stu.

"Why do we have to do dishes? Isn't that what we brought the *niggers* for? After all they've spent years training for this type of work!"

Jamal spun around and grabbed Rush by the hair on the back of his head.

"What's that you're saying, cracker?"

Rush howled in pain as Jamal twisted the handful of hair.

"Hey, lay off him," Stu said, but he backed away after seeing the cold fury on Jamal's face.

"What's going on, fellas?" Professor Reese asked, drawn by the commotion.

"This country cracker was just sharing his viewpoint on what, in his words, is '*nigger* work.' I didn't hear him clearly, so I was asking him if he wouldn't mind repeating it," Jamal answered, tightening his grip. Rush continued to howl and struggled to pry Jamal's fingers loose.

Professor Walker joined Reese in the doorway.

"Let him go, Jamal," he demanded. Jamal hesitated and then relaxed his grip. Rush pulled away and glared at Jamal, while gingerly massaging the back of his scalp.

"Now I take it you two gentlemen know the way to the Peace Tent?" Walker asked. "Because that's where you're going to resolve this."

As they headed for the door, Jamal turned back to the two professors.

"You're wasting your time if you think this is going to solve anything. This retreat is one big waste of time," he told them and then stormed after Rush.

Outside, Rush shoved aside the canvas flap of the Peace Tent and stomped in, muttering and swearing under his breath. He whirled around after Jamal entered and the two of them glared at each other.

"Proud of yourself, you prick?" Rush asked. "It's your fault we're stuck in here, you know."

"I'm just thrilled," Jamal scoffed. "It's my dream to be stuck in these close quarters with a redneck like you. How about you stay over there, I'll stay over here, and in a few minutes we'll go out and pretend like it's all better."

"Too afraid to settle it like a man?" Rush sneered, his fists raised.

"As tempting as that sounds, I'd rather get the hell out of here," Jamal said. "Now shut your mouth so I won't have to shut it for you. You don't have your frat brothers to help you out this time, you racist jerk."

"I don't need them to take you, homey."

"Kiss my ass," Jamal said, moving to the far side of the tent.

They kept their distance from each other for several minutes until Rush started pacing nervously back and forth.

"Can't you sit still?" Jamal asked irritably.

Rush sat on the edge of a folding chair, but his hands wouldn't stop twitching and his feet kept up a constant jitter. Jamal's older brother had been like that—constantly moving, twitching and pacing when he was strung out on coke.

"That white girl is kicking your ass, isn't it?" he asked Rush.

"What the hell you talking about?"

"Don't play me for stupid. I know a cokehead when I see one."

"I don't know what the hell you're talking about."

"Yeah, right. Just like you had nothing to do with that cross burning, right, slick?"

"You're crazy!" Rush snapped and hastily left the tent.

Jamal watched Rush storm off toward the men's cabins. He figured the group would be starting the evening session soon but he wasn't quite ready to join them. He needed some time alone—to cool down and to process Rush's apparent coke addition. Maybe he'd catch up for the evening session. Maybe not.

## CHAPTER EIGHTEEN

With the dishes done, the students took a quick tour of the campgrounds. The campsite overlooked a beautiful lake, circled by hiking and biking trails and sheltered by towering, white pine trees. The main building featured several smaller meeting rooms, the dining hall and the Great Hall. The cabins were spacious yet rustic, and separated by basketball courts.

A central clearing ringed with bleachers was used for meetings and campfires. Closer to the lakeshore was an area reserved for horseshoes, volleyball and football. A large storage shed near the lake held sporting equipment, rowboats and canoes. The distant sound of whippoorwills and the star-filled night created a beautiful backdrop as the tour continued. Tranquility washed over the students who were receptive to letting it in.

"Is it just me, or do things seem simpler out here?" Ashante asked Gloria as the tour neared its end.

Gloria was reminded of how hopeful she had felt while walking along the lake path near Dr. Oliver's cabin. But here, something felt different. She gave Ashante a weak smile. "My momma always said, it's easier to lie down at night when you know what's on the other side of the door in the morning," she said. "This place really does feel peaceful, but I'm still afraid to hope too much."

At seven-thirty the students gathered once again in the Great Hall. Dr. Oliver called for silence.

"Blacks continue to be the most segregated group in this society and remain the most frequent victims of racial prejudice," he began. "You've seen a blatant example of this in the cross burning at your campus. That may seem insignificant to some of you. But you need to consider what that cross symbolized. Think about the violence, rage and fear that consumed the South in the

1960s. Think about the hateful history of such groups as the Ku Klux Klan and the Skinheads. What may have appeared to some of you as merely burning wood actually carried with it the weight of that painful past. A cross burning is one of the most egregious acts that someone can inflict on a fellow human being."

Oliver paused to gauge the effect of his words. "How do you feel when you see footage on television of people in other countries burning our flag? Outraged, right?"

Many students murmured their agreement.

"That's because our flag isn't just a piece of cloth. It is a symbol. It evokes emotions. It's something we hold close to our heart. When someone desecrates it, it feels personal. Well, a burning cross is also a symbol. It represents hatred, oppression, violence and prejudice. For many of us, the American flag stirs up feelings of pride and patriotism. To blacks, a burning cross stirs up wrenching fear and anger. It's personal."

Dr. Oliver beckoned for Gloria to join him at the front of the room. "I've asked Gloria Wilson to share with you just how personal it is."

He grasped Gloria's hand in a warm handshake. His firm grip steadied her nerves.

"The first thing I thought when I saw the flames was that our house was on fire," Gloria told the students, "and that really scared me. But when I realized what it really was, I was even more scared. If it had been a house fire, we would have been devastated, but at least there would have been a logical explanation—faulty wiring, a candle left burning, the iron left on, something. We could have understood why it happened. We could have cleaned up the mess and bought new things to replace what we lost."

Gloria's voice, although soft, had an underlying strength that held everyone's attention.

"Instead, we were left with a different kind of damage and no easy answers," she said. "Someone decided to burn a cross in our

111

yard for no apparent reason other than the fact that we are black. I cannot find the words to tell you how outraged, how sickened, I felt that night. I still feel that way. It was the first time that I personally was the target of such hatred based on my skin color. I know it took place in the 60's in places like Mississippi. We've all read the history and still see terrible acts of racism on the news. But it was always happening to someone else. Then it was in my front yard. I felt the heat. I smelled the smoke. Most of all, I could feel the hatred behind it all, like someone had reached out and torn my heart into pieces." She choked and looked straight at Ashante, whose firm posture gave her an inner strength.

"I have never felt so violated in my life. Although no one laid a hand on me, I felt fractured and scarred. That kind of damage can't be washed away. It's not out here where you can see it; it's in here," she said, pointing to her heart. "The things I have lost—trust, optimism, even my own naiveté—can't be replaced with a quick trip to the store. They can never be recovered entirely."

"Now, for the first time in my life, I feel the power of Langston Hughes' words when he wrote, 'Hold fast to dreams, for if dreams die, life is a broken-winged bird that cannot fly.' It's not that my parents didn't tell me horrific stories about the pain and violence they faced. But they raised us to believe in a better future than they experienced. And it did seem better until I saw the burning cross. Some people say, 'welcome to the real world, G.W.,' but I say, if this is the real world, then it really sucks. Something has to be done, and in a hurry."

Gloria paused for a moment to collect her thoughts and then continued, her voice more subdued. "Some of the worst parts happened after the flames were put out. The cops made Ashante and me feel like we deserved this. We believe the administration knows who did it, but they aren't taking any action. You don't know how it feels unless you've been on this end of it," she said, with a tremor in her voice. "You don't know what it's like to no longer feel like an equal, to feel hated. I didn't know, either, until that night. Now I know. And I can tell you this—it hurts. My heart is no longer whole."

Gloria scanned the faces before her. Ashante's eyes revealed a loving and empathetic understanding. Chuck offered a thumbs-up. When she looked at Dan Trent, she was surprised to see tears in his eyes.

"But I'm tired of feeling like a victim. That's why I'm here," she said, her voice gaining strength. "I don't want anyone else to feel the way I felt that night. Maybe one person can't change the world, but I'm going to do everything in my power to change my corner of it."

Dr. Oliver put his arm around her. The applause started, led by Ashante and Chuck, and then spread around the circle until the room was engulfed with the sound. After the applause died down, Dr. Oliver asked everyone to form a circle. He asked Gloria to stand in the middle of the circle with her eyes closed.

"Beginning with you," Oliver said, pointing to Chris Polaski, "I want each of you to come up one by one and whisper something positive in Gloria's ear. What you say is for her ears only. We won't discuss what is said. When you're done, please go back to your seat."

"That was very powerful. You are one courageous lady," Chris whispered in Gloria's ear. "I love you, G.W. You spoke for both of us. Thank you," Ashante whispered.

Sometimes she recognized the voices and sometimes she didn't, but as the students took their turns, Gloria's face glowed with the positive effect of their words.

Next there was a male voice in her ear, speaking in a halting whisper. "I'm so sorry, G.W.," he said. "I tried to tell you. Mea culpa, mea culpa."

Gloria's heart jumped. Had she heard that right? She wasn't sure, but she thought it sounded like Dan. She realized with a jolt that it sounded exactly like the person who had called to apologize the night of the cross burning. And those words! *Mea culpa, mea culpa.* Gloria fought the urge to open her eyes, but she remembered what Dr. Oliver had said, how the anonymity encouraged people to speak honestly.

She was so distracted that she didn't realize Donna had stepped up to take her turn. *They're here*, she thought; *someone in this room knows what happened that night.* Quietly, Gloria began to sob. Donna had just finished whispering in Gloria's ear, so everyone thought Donna had caused Gloria's tears. Donna looked puzzled as she took her place back in the circle.

When the exercise ended, a hushed silence filled the room. Dr. Oliver asked the rest of the students to close their eyes and join hands. He told them a story about a lost little boy.

"The boy's parents looked for him but were unsuccessful," Oliver related. "Their yard backed up to a wooded area, so it was easy for the boy to get lost. The parents rounded up their friends and neighbors, and everyone searched the woods individually, trying to locate the child. But they were unsuccessful. Then someone suggested that everyone should form one long line, hold hands, and search slowly. They did this, and soon they located the boy. But it was too late. He had died from exposure. One of the searchers remarked, 'I wish we would have thought about joining hands sooner. We could have prevented this tragedy'."

The silence in the room deepened as the message sank in.

"Now you may open your eyes," Oliver said, breaking the students' quiet concentration. "I want you to take a stretch break and join me back here in fifteen minutes."

The students were grateful to be released from the emotional ride. While some headed for the bathrooms, others stepped out for some fresh air. Gloria searched the room for Dan. Their eyes locked and regret filled his face. Gloria wanted to be sure he was the one who had apologized. She headed toward him, but Donna blocked her path.

"Did I say something wrong?" Donna asked. "I didn't mean to make you cry."

Before Gloria could answer, others gathered around to compliment her on her speech.

"Gloria, we're going to find out who did this."

"Don't worry, girl."

"We're with you on this all the way."

Gloria looked around to see if Dan was still in the room and saw him standing in a far corner, talking to Dr. Oliver. Dan looked upset. *Maybe I should wait,* Gloria thought. A few minutes later, Dr. Oliver called the students back to their seats.

"Is there anyone who would like to say a few words either about the cross burning, specifically, or about racial tension at Lakeside, in general?" he asked.

Chris Polaski raised his hand and stepped to the center of the circle. He pushed his hands deep into his pockets to hide their shaking, but the slight tremor in his voice revealed his nervousness.

"I don't have a speech prepared or anything," he said softly, "but I do have some stuff I want to say. I don't want to make anyone mad, though." He glanced at Dr. Oliver for assurance.

"The purpose of this retreat is for everyone to have a chance to be heard," Oliver said. "As long as you're not attacking anyone personally, say exactly what's on your mind."

Chris nodded and swallowed hard, keeping his eyes glued to the floor.

"Well, don't get me wrong. I feel bad about what happened to Gloria and Ashante. I mean, they seem real nice and everything, and they certainly didn't deserve what happened. Whoever it was that did it, they're a bunch of first-rate jerks in my book, and they deserve to be nailed to the wall for it."

"But what I want to say is, it really pisses me off that because of what a couple of idiots did, now all of us white students are treated like we're guilty, too. I made a comment that night that it was probably just a prank because I didn't want anyone to feel personally attacked. Not here at Lakeside. I didn't want to believe it. In hindsight, I guess I shouldn't have said it, but Chuck over there nearly took my head off."

"I've never in my life had a problem with anyone because of their race. But now all of a sudden, it's us against them. Now I'm the enemy just because I'm white. The truth is, I'm tired of feeling guilty because a white plantation owner owned slaves in Georgia in the 1800's. I wasn't there. My relatives weren't there. I'm Polish. My ancestors on my dad's side lived in New York. They fought for the North in the Civil War—fought to get rid of slavery."

"They suffered all kinds of ethnic slurs. So did my grandparents and parents. It still happens to me today—you know, the dumb Pollock jokes—so I get it. Yet most of the time when I'm around black people, I feel like they're waiting for an apology."

Chris's voice cracked with emotion. The silence in the room was electric.

"Some of my mom's relatives were killed in the gas chambers by the Nazis during the Holocaust," he continued. "But you don't see me blaming every German person I meet. The point I'm trying to make is, don't judge us all based on what a few of us do. If I had known they were going to burn that cross, I would have tried to stop it, but I had no clue. I'm really sorry for Gloria and Ashante. But just because some ignorant rednecks are showing off their inbred mentality, it doesn't mean we have to turn it into a campus-wide racial crisis." Chris shrugged and managed a smile. "That's about it, I guess," he said. "I just needed to get that off my chest."

"Thanks, Chris," Dr. Oliver said. "It takes courage to speak your mind."

The students applauded. But as Chris started to sit back down, Dr. Oliver held up a hand. "Before you sit, Chris, I think this is a good opportunity for a very quick, but very important, vocabulary lesson. I have heard many of you say that accusations of 'racism' have been thrown around quite a lot on your campus lately. And we're soon going to dive headfirst into what that looks like. But before we do, I want to talk about the word itself. And Chris, your very impassioned comments can help us do just that."

Chris looked nervous as Dr. Oliver made his way around the room. He came to stop in front of Lori Christianson. "Ms. Christianson," he said, "what does the word 'racism' mean?"

Lori glanced at Gloria and, in a hesitant voice, said, "Well, it's when someone treats someone else in a negative way, based on their race."

Dr. Oliver smiled. "Lori, that's a perfectly succinct definition of 'discrimination.' Now dig a little deeper: What's behind that treatment? What's motivating the person who's discriminating?"

Lori frowned. "Um, hate, I guess? Fear? I think sometimes people do really stupid things based on race, just because they're afraid—they've probably never known anybody of a different race before."

Oliver nodded. "Yes," he said, "often hate and fear are very powerful motivators." He strolled along for another few paces before coming to a stop in front of Mark Serra.

"Mr. Serra," he said. "What do you think? What is racism?"

"I think it's like a lot of other 'isms'," Mark said. "I think it stems from power."

"Ah! An interesting choice of words, Mr. Serra," Dr. Oliver said. "How do you mean?"

"Well, racism is like homophobia—," but before he could go on, Kwame and Chuck let out loud groans.

"No way, man!" Kwame said, rolling his eyes.

"Wait," Dr. Oliver said. "I think it's best we hear Mark out. Mr. Serra?"

"What I was saying," Mark said, "is that homophobia and sexism and racism—they all depend on one group having more power in a society than another group. And then benefiting from it, like privilege. Like white privilege, or straight privilege. As a white person, I know I'm privileged in ways I don't even realize, every single day. But I'll tell you—," he paused to look at Chuck and Kwame, "—I see every day how straight people are privileged too. So, while I definitely don't understand what it's like to be black, I get what it's like to be part of a group that's thought less of, for reasons that have nothing to do with who we really are."

"Good—thank you," Dr. Oliver said as he strolled back to the front of the room, where Chris still stood.

"So, we've identified a couple of things," Dr. Oliver said. "First, the individual acts of hatred—or, personal racism, as Ms. Christianson helped us define. And second, something called 'institutional racism,' which gets at the power and privilege Mr. Serra so eloquently described. Now I'd like to answer my own question, and tell you my definitions of racism, which are the definitions we'll be using for the rest of our time together."

"First, personal racism can be understood as the hatred or intolerance of another race, grounded in the belief that one's own race is superior."

Dr. Oliver waited a moment to let his words sink in. He glanced at Chris and was pleased to see a look of deep thought on the young man's face. Then he continued. "And second, institutional racism is this. Now listen carefully, because this is always the harder one to understand. Institutional racism can be understood as the systematic distribution of resources, power and opportunity in our society, to the benefit of people who are white, and to the exclusion of people of color."

He repeated the definition, and again he waited. After a few moments, he turned to Chris. "Mr. Polaski," he said. "I think you demonstrated in your comments earlier that you very likely do not hate black people. Is that correct?"

Chris looked taken aback. "Of course I don't!" he said.

"I'm curious," Dr. Oliver asked, "what do you make of our second definition? Do you hear anything in it that sounds familiar, given your family's history?"

Slowly, Chris nodded. "Exclusion," he said. "My ancestors were excluded from participating as full members of society. And they were absolutely denied, what did you call it—resources and opportunities."

"I imagine they were," Dr. Oliver said. "Did you know there was a time in U.S. history when Polish, Irish and Italian immigrants weren't considered fully 'white'? They were denied the same rights and privileges as other white people. Chris, you described earlier how that made you feel. So it seems you have more in common with the African American students on your campus than you thought you did."

"I never really thought about it like that before," Chris said, clearly moved.

Dr. Oliver smiled. "Chris, my friend, you may take your seat."

As Chris made his way back to his chair, Chuck reached out his hand and stopped him. Chris started to back away warily, but then noticed Chuck's smile.

"Hey man," Chuck said. "I just wanted to say, about that night—well, I'm sorry. I was out of line, getting on your case. I was just blowin' off steam." Chuck offered Chris his hand. "What do you say? Are we cool?"

Chris relaxed and grasped Chuck's hand. "We're cool," he said. "Maybe we can shoot a few hoops later or something."

"I'll wipe the court with you, player," Chuck said, grinning.

Dr. Oliver noted the exchange but he knew better than to call attention to it.

"Chris brought up a legitimate concern," he told the group. "Some of you may be asking similar questions. Is this being blown out of proportion? Was it, as your administrators insist, just a harmless prank? Well, my response to that is: When they burned that cross, it became anything but harmless. There's too much history connected to that image, too much pain. But having said that, some of the things that have happened don't fit with a purely racial motive."

"What do you mean?" Ashante asked.

"Any administration would have much more to lose from appearing to support racism than from condemning it. Something doesn't add up. And with your help we're going to get to the bottom of it this weekend."

"How?" Chuck asked.

"We continue to communicate and sort through what we've learned so far. Some of the exercises we do this weekend may seem irrelevant or silly, but I assure you that the more we communicate, the easier it will be to trust one another. That trust will ultimately lead us to the truth."

"Then what are we waitin' for, sir?" Chuck grinned.

"That's the spirit!" Oliver replied. "What I need you to do now is divide into four groups. I want an equal mix of men and women, blacks and whites."

As the students milled around the room, Jamal and Rush came in.

"You're just in time," Oliver greeted the two. "Find yourselves a spot in one of these groups."

Jamal slid in next to Kwame.

"What's your song, King Kong? How was life in the pup tent?" Kwame teased.

"Interesting. I got some dirt on good old Rush."

"What's that?"

"He's strung out."

"No, shit?"

"Word. So what did I miss?"

"Dr. Oliver thinks the whole cross burning thing might have been a set-up."

"What!"

"Relax, bro. He just thinks there may be more to this than meets the eye, and he raised some very interesting questions."

"Like what?"

Dr. Oliver gave them a pointed glance, and they quickly fell silent.

"Now, drawing upon the two definitions we discussed, I want each group to brainstorm a list of racial problems that students face at Lakeside," Oliver instructed. "Choose a spokesperson and have him or her write the problems down on these sheets of paper."

The room filled with the buzz of voices. Ashante wrote for her group and had a hard time keeping up with the flurry of suggestions.

"Wait a minute," she interrupted, flexing her cramped fingers. "Racial... I'm still writing...profiling?"

In the next group, Donna jotted down the problems in flowery penmanship. Chuck was in her group, and he noticed that she quickly recorded every word he uttered, so he started repeating what the other students wanted voiced.

Jamal quickly took leadership of his group. And Bruce, who was chosen unanimously despite protesting that his handwriting was illegible, led the fourth group.

"Time's up," said Oliver, calling a halt to the brainstorming. He instructed each group to review its list and select one problem to share with the full room.

"We will collect all the lists, compile them, and then distribute the master list at a later date, so hopefully all of the issues will receive some attention," he told the students, "but for now, let's just concentrate on one issue from each group."

"We chose racial harassment," Ashante announced. "That includes stuff like the cross burning and other stuff like stereotyping and discrimination. We think that's a huge problem because it sets people apart and makes them likely targets."

Jamal went next. "Our issue is that faculty and administrators often have different expectations depending on the race of a student," he said, abandoning some of his more militant topics and going with the group consensus for once. "There also is a definite lack of professors from different ethnic groups, which only makes the problem worse."

"We think a big problem at Lakeside is the lack of social interaction between black and white students," Donna said when it was her turn. "We're together in class, but as soon as class is out, we divide up by race and go our separate ways. We need to mingle more."

Bruce squinted at his scribbled notes, to the amusement of his group. "Well, if I can read what I've written here, our issue is the real lack of ethnic studies and opportunities at Lakeside for minorities," he said.

"Okay," Oliver said, as he finished writing the four issues on the blackboard. "These are our four points of attack then. Let's look at each one in turn, and see if we can come up with a few examples to better illustrate them. For racial harassment, the cross burning has already been mentioned. What are some other examples?"

"Stereotyping," Ashante said. "Like assuming all black guys are gang members and all black girls are going to get pregnant before they're married."

"Good," Oliver said. "What else?"

"Racial slurs," Lori said. "People call each other the meanest, most degrading things, and a lot of it is racially motivated."

"Like what?"

"I'd rather not say," Lori said, blushing.

"Oh, come on," Chuck said. "We've all heard them—coon, monkey, *nigger.*"

"Fag, gay blade, limp wrist," Mark Serra added.

"Spic, greaser."

"Gook."

"Slant eyes, slope head."

"Wop."

"Scrub."

"Wigger wannabe."

The words formed a chant as the students took turns calling them out.

"Okay, I think we get the point," Oliver said. "These aren't just harmless words! When they're aimed at an individual with the venom and hatred that usually accompanies them, they carry a lot more sting."

He directed the students' attention to the different expectations from faculty and administrators.

"I have a good example of that," Chuck said. "Just because I play football, everyone assumes that's the only way I made it to college. They expect me to be a dumb jock. When I registered for classes as a freshman, I wanted to take zoology, but my faculty advisor, a white guy, acted like I was out of my mind. He kept saying how that was too much of a workload with the labs and stuff. He said I should take a lighter course load so it wouldn't be too much during football season."

"I told him I was there for an education, not just to play ball. He basically told me I'd just end up dropping the class, so not to waste my time or his. I know a lot of the white guys on the team signed up for classes with labs and heavy workloads, and no one seemed to have a problem with that. I switched advisors, to Ms. Jones, who's black. I took zoology and got a B+."

"Very good example, Chuck. Now that we have an idea of what we're up against, I want you to think of some solutions for these problems," Oliver said. "Tomorrow we'll divide up into new groups and do some more brainstorming to see what we can come up with.

"We've taken the most important step. We've opened a dialogue. Communication is the key. Whatever you do after this retreat, you have to keep talking to each other. There are no easy fixes to the problems you are facing on your campus. You cannot solve all your problems in one weekend, but you can learn problem-solving skills. Once you're back at Lakeside, you'll know how to tackle other issues as they arise."

"More importantly," Oliver continued, "is that as college students you have a great opportunity—no a responsibility—to learn about who you are, and your connection to the broader, outside world. Take advantage of your college tenure to expand your worldview and how you relate to others."

He glanced around the room; students sagged in their seats, clearly exhausted. "Well folks, it's been a long day. We're off to a good start, but what do you say we call it a night? It's ten p.m., so you've got a couple hours of free time. Remember, though, morning comes early, and we have a long day ahead of us."

## CHAPTER NINETEEN

A s the students exited the hall, Dr. Oliver took Gloria aside.

"You may want to catch up with Dan and try talking to him," he said.

"I had planned on it," Gloria said. "I saw you talking with him before. Dr. Oliver—I think he apologized to me in the circle. Did he tell you that? Do you think he could be the one who burned the cross?"

Dr. Oliver shook his head. "I don't really know. But he seems quite upset. He didn't tell me anything specific, but he asked me to set aside time tomorrow so he can speak to the group as a whole. He said he wanted to explain things to you first, though. He's obviously struggling with something."

"He actually seems like a decent guy. Do you really think—?"

But Dr. Oliver cut in. "I think you should ask him that," he said gently. "He just walked outside."

Gloria gave Dr. Oliver a grateful smile and headed for the door. Outside the Great Hall, students milled around the yard. Gloria noticed a couple of guys heading toward the basketball court, and another group talking and laughing around one of the picnic tables.

Gloria scanned the clearing and spotted Dan leaning against a far tree, removed from all the others. He was staring in the direction of the Great Hall, and for a brief moment, Gloria thought Dan was looking right at her. She felt her pulse quicken—*was he waiting for her? Will he tell me who's responsible for the cross burning?* She had to talk to him so she waved to get his attention.

Their eyes met, and though Gloria tried to give him a reassuring smile, he abruptly straightened and turned to walk away.

*Just great*, Gloria thought, and she began to hurry after him. Before she could get much farther than the picnic table, Jamal called out to her.

"Hey," he said, "how did your talk go?"

"Oh, all right, I guess," she said. She looked around—*where had Dan gone?* She caught sight of him heading toward the path that led to the cabins.

"Just all right?" Jamal asked. "You sound upset—something bugging you?"

"No, I'm fine. I'm just in a hurry. I've got to catch up with Dan."

\*\*\*

Jamal watched Gloria dash away. Well, that was strange, he thought. In fact, he wasn't sure which was stranger—Gloria's sudden interest in Dan, or the fact that he was bothered by her apparent disinterest in him. He was considering going after her when Kwame and Chuck walked up.

"Hey, man," Kwame said. "What's up?"

"Nothing," Jamal said, still looking in Gloria's retreating direction.

Together they watched as Gloria tried to catch up with Dan, on the dimly lit path leading to the cabins.

"Whoa," Kwame said.

"What the hell!" Chuck said. "What's Gloria up to?"

Jamal shook his head. "Your guess is as good as mine, bro."

"I bet it has to do with whatever Dan said to her in the circle," Kwame said. "I think he's the one who made her cry. As soon as he sat back down, it looked like he was going to bawl, too!"

"What do you mean, he made her cry?" Jamal said. "What did he say to her?"

"I don't know, but I plan on asking him later," Kwame said. Then he grinned. "What, all of a sudden you care about G.W.'s feelings? I thought you weren't into her. That damn peace tent must have straightened your ass out, huh?"

Jamal rolled his eyes, and both Chuck and Kwame started to laugh. "Whatever," Jamal said. "Come on, I thought we were gonna shoot some hoops," he said, quickly changing the subject.

"Let's go," Kwame said as they headed off to the court. "By the way-so how do you know Rush is strung out? Did you beat a confession out of him?"

"Nothing that drastic," Jamal said, relieved to be talking about something other than Gloria. "But I know a blow freak when I see one."

"That punk's using?" Chuck asked.

Jamal nodded. "He was all wigged out—fast talking, twitching, couldn't sit still and constantly looking around. You know how he won't part with those stupid shades? That's because his eyes are glowing like stoplights. He rubs his nose constantly. I thought he was going to take a hit right in front of me."

They walked up to the basketball court and found Chris and Bruce shooting free throws.

"Hey, hippie," Chuck yelled, "mind if we join you?"

Bruce turned with a smile. "Come on, if you think you can take the heat, player."

"Got room for one more?" another voice called out. They turned and saw Mark, wearing a beat-up pair of gym shorts and an old *Chicago Bulls* T-shirt.

Jamal bit his tongue to keep from laughing. But he couldn't help the surprise in his voice. "You?" he said, as Chuck and Kwame gawked.

"Yeah," Mark said, "believe it or not, a gay guy can play basketball. Imagine that!" Mark softened his sarcasm with a wide grin. He took the ball from Chris and sank it from three-point range.

"Nice shot," Kwame said, jumping in to retrieve the rebound.

"It's all in the wrist," Mark answered with a laugh. After a moment the others joined in laughing, too.

"You're all right, you know that?" Kwame said. "As long as you keep sinking shots like that, you can be on my team. Just don't hog the ball, white boy!"

The guys were soon caught up in the heat of the game, as they elbowed their way under the boards.

## CHAPTER TWENTY

After about an hour the basketball game petered out. Jamal and Chris shot a game of horse, while Mark and Kwame sprawled on the grass and watched. Chuck decided to go look for more exciting entertainment and headed toward the women's cabins.

He followed the sound of female voices to Gloria and Lori's room, where several girls were lounging around, talking and playing board games. Chuck waved to Gloria and then scanned the room, finding Donna digging through a cooler near the doorway.

"Got anything in there for a thirsty guy like me?" he asked, approaching her. Donna dropped her soda in surprise. She snatched the can up and hastily opened it, accidentally spraying both herself and Chuck with foam.

"Whoa, can I get it in a glass?" Chuck said, wiping his face.

"Oh jeez, I'm sorry," Donna said. "Here, let me get you a towel."

"No, it's okay," Chuck said. "I needed a shower after my game anyway."

They stood and stared at each other awkwardly for a moment, and then they both grinned.

"Would you like to go for a walk or something?" Chuck said.

Donna hesitated.

"Come on, consider it homework," he said. "You're the one who said a big problem on campus is the lack of social interaction. 'We need to mingle more,' I believe were your exact words. So what do you say? Are you up for some mingling? It'll give us a jumpstart on solving that problem!"

Donna smiled, and her heart pounded. "All right. Just let me grab a sweatshirt from my room," she said. They stepped out into the cool, night air and walked in silence, listening to the sounds of the crickets and the frogs chirping and croaking in the reeds along the lake. After a long moment of silence, they both started to talk at once.

Chuck laughed. "Sorry, you go ahead," he said.

"No, really. What were you going to say?"

"I was just going to ask what you think of the retreat so far."

"I think it's really neat," Donna said. Immediately, she grimaced. "God, that's lame, isn't it? I swear, sometimes I just open my mouth and say the stupidest things. You probably think I'm just another airhead blonde, don't you? Now I'm talking too much. Sorry. Shut up, Donna."

Chuck tried not to laugh as she chastised herself.

"Relax, woman," he said. "I won't bite. I nibble a little, but only gently."

Donna blushed. "Sorry. I'm just a little nervous. This is the first time I've ever been alone..."

"Alone, with what? A black guy?" Chuck asked, amused.

"No, that's not what I meant. I was going to say I don't usually make a habit of wandering around in the woods at night with someone I hardly know."

"You have nothing to fear, darling," Chuck said, stretching his voice into a fairly accurate southern drawl. "I'll be a perfect gentleman." A mischievous gleam appeared in his eye. "Unless, of course, you'd rather..."

"That's all right," Donna said hastily. In her confusion, she stumbled over a tree branch strewn across the path. As she tipped forward, Chuck reached out and grabbed her hand and helped her keep her balance. His touch sent an electric current up her arm.

He felt her shiver. "Are you cold?" he asked.

"A little, I guess," she said.

Chuck let go of her hand and slipped an arm around her waist. "Well, we'll have to see what we can do to warm you up."

Chuck's aftershave mingled with the faint smell of sweat, and Donna's pulse quickened.

"You asked what I think of this retreat," she said, trying to keep her voice from cracking. "And I guess I have to say, I'm really enjoying it. I thought the discussion tonight was really productive, and I think Dr. Oliver is a fascinating man, don't you? And, of course, I thought Gloria was very effective. Every time I hear her talk about that night, I get so angry—."

Chuck didn't let her finish. Instead, he pulled her close and kissed her hard on the mouth.

But Donna quickly pulled away. "What did you do that for?" she asked, pressing her hand over her mouth.

"It was the only way I could think of to get you to stop talking," Chuck said. "Besides, I thought that's what you wanted."

"Why would you think that?"

"I don't know. The way you've been looking at me and coming on to me all day," Chuck said, reaching for her again. "All my friends noticed. You gonna honestly try and tell me you came out here with me to talk about Dr. Oliver and racial issues?"

"I...I don't know," Donna said. "I wasn't coming on to you all day! At least, not really. I just thought you seemed nice."

"And now what? Now I'm not so nice? Hey, girl, I see what I want, and I go for it. Don't go all cold on me now."

He tried to pull her close again, but Donna shoved him with both hands and broke away. "I said no—not like this," she said.

Suddenly the mix of sweat and aftershave wasn't exciting at all. Her eyes filled with tears, and she reached up to wipe them away. "I thought you were a decent guy. But clearly I made a mistake."

"Oh, really," he said, his anger growing. "I bet if I was some rich, white, frat boy, you'd be more than willing. What's the matter? You afraid a little black will stain your lily whiteness?"

"I won't let you talk to me like this," Donna said. Her tears had turned to an anger of her own. "I really thought better of you,

Chuck. Thanks for showing me the real you." With that, she turned and ran, stumbling back toward the cabin.

Chuck watched her go. As she disappeared through the trees, he lashed out at a fallen tree branch, kicking it out of his way.

"What the hell?" he said under his breath. "One minute she's hot, the next she's as frigid as a polar bear's ass."

He headed back to the basketball court. Chris was the only one there.

"Hey, player," Chuck said. "Where's everyone else?"

"They crashed."

"Up for some one-on-one?"

"Sure thing."

They played in silence for several moments, jostling for the rebounds.

"So, how'd it go?" Chris asked.

"What do you mean?"

"With Donna. Kwame said you were going to see how far you could get. Bum-rush, he said."

"What, you guys didn't have anything better to do than discuss my love life?"

"Hey, don't get touchy. I was just curious."

"Sorry. It's just, well, women. You know how they are."

"Yeah, actually I'm an expert," Chris said, trying to get Chuck to lighten up. "But seriously if you want to talk about it, I'm willing to listen."

"Who are you, Dr. Phil?" Chuck snapped.

"Okay, forget I asked. Try decaf next time, man. You're way too intense for me to deal with."

Chris dropped the basketball and turned to leave, but Chuck stopped him.

"Wait, man. Maybe you can help," Chuck said. "I really fucked up."

They sat along the edge of the court as Chuck told Chris what happened.

"White women!" Chuck said, barely hiding his disappointment. "Man, they piss me off. They make a brother think they're all hot for him; but when it comes right down to it, they play these bullshit games."

"I know Donna pretty well, and she's not like that," Chris said. "It sounds like you came with a full-court press before you gave her a chance to finish warm-ups. Then, when she tried to slow things down, you assumed it was because of your skin color. Don't get pissed at me for saying this, Chuck, but you're way too ready to read racism into everything white people say and do. Guys come on too strong all the time. She has the right to say *no*, you know what I mean? It's not a black and white thing, man. You just got ahead of yourself."

"But she was coming on to me all day."

"Do you, what's the word – 'bum-rush'—every woman that hard?"

"No, but this was different."

"Why?"

"Because she's, um—you wouldn't understand," Chuck said, lamely.

"Because she's white. That's what you were going to say isn't it? It was a race thing! Only you were the one doing it, not her!"

"I knew you wouldn't get it. I can't explain it. All the brothers saw the way she was coming on to me, so I thought it would be an easy lay."

"And maybe you came on stronger than usual because you wanted to impress your friends?"

Surprising himself, Chuck managed to control his temper long enough to realize Chris had a valid point.

"What should I do?" he asked Chris quietly.

"I think you should try telling her the truth. What have you got to lose?"

"Word. You know Chris, you're all right. Of course, if you tell anyone about this, I'll have to open a can of whip-ass on you."

"I wouldn't expect anything less," Chris said with a grin.

## CHAPTER TWENTY ONE

The next morning, Dr. Oliver looked refreshed and ready to take on the world. After breakfast, he waited by the door as the students filed into the Great Hall and greeted each one by name.

As a warm-up, Dr. Oliver instructed the students to don blindfolds. Without speaking, he said, they needed to create a biracial circle, alternating black and white. The students moved about in confusion, bumping into one another, exchanging handshakes, feeling each other's clothing, and even rubbing each other's hair, as they tried to determine where they should stand. By the time the circle was complete, everyone was laughing and out of breath, and the day was off to a good start.

Next, the group watched a video called, *College Racism 101*, which explored racial incidents on college campuses. When the tape finished, Dr. Oliver opened the floor for discussion. "Do you think racism is a serious problem at Lakeside?" he said.

"I do," Lori said, "but it's not as bad as the universities we saw in that film. I mean, there's the one incident of the cross burning, but nothing else as drastic."

"That doesn't mean the problem is any less serious," Jamal interjected. "The film talked primarily about individual racist acts. What I'm more concerned about is institutional racism, although I could cite you examples of individual acts of racism that blacks experience every single day.

"But there's never been an analysis of how institutional racism continues to create inequity and suffering, and how our institutions support it. The cross burning, as far as I'm concerned, is symptomatic of this larger problem. It's a sign of things to come. The fact that our administration is willing to look the other way shows me no one is safe at Lakeside."

Ashante leaned forward in her chair, her brow furrowed in thought. "I don't think it should have to come to something like a cross burning before racism is considered a problem," she said. "We need to deal with this at the roots. The more I think about it, the more I realize the signs were there that something like this could happen at Lakeside. The whispers, the racial slurs, the moment when you walk into a room of white students and they all stop talking. I just ignored it all until that night, when it got pushed too far to ignore."

The other black students nodded in agreement.

"I would agree with that," Mark said.

"Yeah, me, too," said Donna. She sat between Lori and Gloria, sitting as far as possible from Chuck, who sat next to Kwame across the room.

"Okay then, what, in your opinions, can be done about it?" Oliver asked. "Do you think it's possible to achieve racial harmony at Lakeside?"

Bruce spoke up first. "Well, I think true racial harmony is a pipe dream, but that doesn't mean we shouldn't work toward achieving as much of it as we can," he said. "It will take an awful lot of work. We have to confront our fears, be honest with each other, and be willing to confront each other, if we're going to make any headway."

"So you feel confrontation is a necessary step?" Dr. Oliver said.

"Yeah," Bruce said, "and probably the hardest one, too."

Dr. Oliver motioned to the rest of the room, his face intense. He was going to push them, he knew; but after the previous night, he thought they were ready for it. "How about the rest of you?" he said. "Do you all think confrontation is necessary?"

The majority of the students nodded *yes*.

"All right then," Dr. Oliver said, rubbing his hands together. "Let's try it! The first step in a confrontation is to put all our cards on the table. So let me begin." He grabbed a piece of chalk and scribbled on the blackboard: *All whites are racist!*

"You, Kwame, what do you think of this statement?" he asked.

Kwame shrugged. "I think it's pretty close to the mark. I've hardly met any white people who weren't racist in some way, although some are worse than others."

Across the room, Lori's hand shot into the air. "Wait, though," she said. "Were they all really racist, or have you just decided all whites are racist, so you interpret their behavior to fit that mold?"

Before Kwame could answer, Rush jumped in. "I say blacks are just as racist as whites, even more so," he said. "They walk around acting like we owe them the world because of stuff that happened two hundred years ago. If they're so miserable here, why don't they get on a boat and sail back to Africa?"

Kwame rolled his eyes and glanced at Lori. "See what I mean?" he said. "Case closed."

"But wait," Stu said. "Rush is right! I bet life in the U.S. of A. doesn't look so bad compared to living in Somalia or Rwanda about now."

Dr. Oliver, who had been watching the conversation in silence, moved back to the blackboard. "Well what about it, Ashante?" he asked. "What do you think of this statement?" He scribbled again with the chalk: *"Blacks should quit blaming whites for their problems and do something about it themselves!"*

Ashante glanced at Jamal before speaking. "Well, actually, I kind of agree with that," she said, slowly. "I think sometimes blacks use our race and our history as a crutch or an excuse for why their lives are a failure. It makes me really mad when I hear guys from my neighborhood blaming their drug habits or their rap sheets on the fact that they're black and that their ancestors were enslaved. That's an insult to our ancestors and all they suffered, in my opinion."

"We each have to take responsibility for ourselves, for our actions today. It's important that we take pride in our cultural heritage and that we not forget our roots, but those things should be steps on a ladder to raise us up, not shackles on our ankles holding us down."

"Wait right there, sister," Jamal interrupted. "Whites are responsible for most of the problems we face today! We're turned down for jobs, for housing, for educational opportunities, all based on our race."

"I know that," Ashante said, forgetting her fear of public speaking. "White people have done, and continue to do, a lot of things that hinder the progress of our people, but I don't see how sitting around pointing fingers solves anything. And climbing on the next boat to Africa is not an option," she added, glaring at Rush and Stu.

"Well, it's not all a piece of cake being a white male in today's job market, you know," Rush shot back, quoting the speech he'd heard from his father hundreds of times. "With all this cockamamie affirmative action crap, companies are forced to hire unqualified minorities and women just to fill their quotas. White males get the shaft!"

"Even if that were true, which it's not, do you think burning crosses will solve the problem?" Jamal asked.

"Are you accusing me of something?" Rush asked, rising to his feet.

"Hey, if the shoe fits," Jamal said, "and it looks like a pretty good fit from here."

"Cool it, fellas," Dr. Oliver said, stepping to the center of the room. "Remember: attack the issue, not the individual."

"Issues didn't burn that cross—he probably did," Jamal replied, furious. "Until that's taken care of, none of this is going to accomplish anything."

"This is not the time or the place," Dr. Oliver told Jamal, quietly but firmly.

"That's the whole problem right there," Jamal shouted. "It's never the right time or place when it comes to holding whites accountable for what they do to us."

Now it was Bruce's turn to interrupt. He leaned toward Jamal and held his palms out. "Hey man, why don't you just chill," Bruce said.

"Shut the hell up!" Jamal yelled at him. "You have no idea what it's like."

"Maybe not," Bruce said. "But all I see is you're pissed off at the whole world, and you're taking it out on everyone around you. It's just making the situation worse."

"Like you're one to talk!" Jamal scowled. "Do you think it helped the situation when you and the rest of your buddies turned on us and started brown-nosing the administration?"

Bruce stood up and took a step toward Jamal. "Who are you calling a brown-noser?" he said.

"Did I offend you? Maybe you'd prefer ass kisser?"

"That's it," Bruce said, slamming his fist against the back of his chair. "You push everything too far. I'm sick of your piss-poor attitude."

"Oh, yeah?" Jamal said, leaping to his feet. "What are you going to do about it?"

"You can both step outside to the Peace Tent," Oliver told them.

Jamal threw up his hands and strode out of the hall. Bruce followed him silently.

"I think that's enough discussion for now," Oliver said, trying to ease the tension. "We've got one hour until lunch—why don't we take a break?"

***

Jamal stormed through the entrance of the Peace Tent and stood with his back to the door and his arms tightly crossed. *That asshole*, he thought. *Every time I let my guard down, he proves he can't be trusted.* When he heard Bruce step in behind him, Jamal whirled around.

"So what's up, you want to throw some hands?" Jamal sneered. "I thought you were all big into this 'give peace a chance' crap, and now all of a sudden you want to fight me?"

Bruce shook his head and looked apologetic. "Back off, man. I don't want to fight you. Not that you couldn't use an attitude adjustment, but that's not why I laid into you. I did it because I needed to get you alone."

"Hey man, I prefer women!" Jamal said, mockingly.

"Cut the crap and listen. This is important. Dr. Oliver isn't the only one who thinks there was more to this than just that damned cross. This whole thing has smelled bad from the beginning. The reason I went along with the Dean is because I knew it would give me the inside track to look into things. As long as they thought I was on their side, they didn't bother to conceal what they were doing—or, rather, not doing—about the whole situation."

Jamal frowned, and his arms loosened. "What are you saying?"

"You're not one for giving anyone a chance to explain, but that's all right. Your anger gave me a perfect cover. You made your low opinion of me quite clear, and the administration was thrilled. They figured since you were so angry with me, there was no way I could be supporting your cause."

Jamal scoffed. "So I'm supposed to believe you've been running around like some kind of Sherlock Holmes, looking to further the cause of brothers everywhere?"

"You can believe what you want, but there's been no official investigation," Bruce said. "But you already assumed that. You may not, however, know the reason. I think there's no investigation, because they don't need one. I'll lay you odds Severson and Horning already knows who did it."

"Who?"

"Unfortunately, most of what I've been able to dig up is circumstantial. But I'm leaning in the direction of Rush and Stu. My friend Steve Walsh found out they were stopped for prowling behind Gloria's house about a week before the cross burning. It's common knowledge that every time those two get into trouble, their parents bail them out with a large donation to Lakeside."

Jamal let out a long, low whistle. "Okay," he said, "I'm listening."

"Lately there have been all kinds of closed-door meetings between the administration and the fathers of those two. I'll bet they leave with their wallets lighter every time. I also overheard a bunch of their frat buddies teasing them about learning their fire building skills in Boy Scouts. And, from what I gather, those two weren't given a choice about attending this retreat."

They lapsed into silence, mulling over the situation.

***

As the students mingled outside during the break, Donna found a quiet spot under a tree and sank to the ground. She watched as the others laughed and talked in small groups, and with a sad smile, she realized many of her peers were beginning to actually enjoy themselves. *I was having fun, too, until last night*, she thought. When she got back to her cabin the night before, she'd made up a story about not feeling well and had gone straight to bed. Now she wondered how she could manage to avoid Chuck and his friends for the rest of the weekend without it being too obvious.

She glanced up just as Chuck and Kwame were leaving the Great Hall. When she saw them begin to walk in her direction, she hastily pulled a paperback from her bag and pretended to read. As they neared, she could hear Chuck tell Kwame to go on without him. She didn't look up from her book, but she could hear the rustling of his shoes against the grass as he came close.

"Mind if I sit down?" he asked.

Donna felt herself wince, but despite herself, she shrugged. He joined her under the tree, maintaining an acceptable distance.

"I've been thinking about last night," Chuck said, "and I guess I came on pretty strong."

*You could say that again*, Donna thought to herself—but she remained silent, biting her lip and staring at her book.

"Listen Donna, I just wanted to tell you I'm really sorry. I know I went too far. I have a little sister, and if anybody treated her the way I treated you last night—well, let's just say they'd be walking funny for weeks. I've been kicking myself for how I acted. All my friends were telling me to go for it, and I let myself get caught up in all their shit, and I shouldn't have. I'm really sorry."

He paused for a moment, and in the silence Donna let those final three words echo around in her head. She'd seen the way Chuck had watched out for Gloria and Ashante the night of the fire, and the way he was always trying to help his friends. At the beginning of the weekend, she'd thought he was a really good guy. His apology certainly sounded believable—so maybe he really was.

"Look, I can tell you want me to leave you alone," Chuck said. "I get that." As he moved to go, Donna looked up and met his gaze for the first time.

"Wait," she said. "I appreciate what you just said. Really. It means something."

"I said things last night that I didn't mean. " Chuck said. "You really do deserve better."

142

Donna nodded; now that Chuck was apologizing, she thought she should probably come clean, too. "Actually," she said, "I've been thinking about something you said last night—something that hit close to home for me. And I've been feeling kind of bad about it."

"Bad? Why would you feel bad?" Chuck said. "I was the one who was out of line."

"Yeah, you were, but you were right about me coming onto you. I was," she said hesitantly, "and it was partially because you're black."

Chuck drew back in surprise. "Come again?"

"It's kind of complicated," she said. "See, my stepdad is black," she said.

"No shit! Really?" Chuck said, his eyes widening.

"Yeah. My father died when I was 13. His best friend was this black guy named Odell. He was there for my mom when she really needed him—he helped make the funeral arrangements, sat with her when she needed to cry, that sort of thing. When mom wouldn't leave the house, Odell told her she needed to be strong for me and my brother.

"After my dad died, my brother went off to the military, and I sort of withdrew into my own little world. So my mom became pretty dependent on Odell, and they started to spend a lot of time together. When they announced they were getting married, I lost it. No one could replace my dad—especially, I'm ashamed to say now, a *black man*."

"Okay," Chuck said slowly, "but what does this have to do with us?"

"I'm getting there," Donna said, smiling. "See, I was so angry that I moved in with my grandparents for the rest of high school. I never really gave Odell a chance, even though he literally saved my mother's life. He called me on each of my birthdays and invited me home for the holidays, but I refused to take his calls.

But then, a year ago my mom was hurt in a car accident. I went home for the first time in a really long time and had a long talk with her. I realized how much she loves Odell. She let me know that he never tried to replace my dad, and that he had always been there for us, even when dad was alive."

Donna paused and frowned. "I know this is a long story, but it helps to share the details. It helps to make sense of things, you know?"

Chuck smiled. "Don't worry," he said. "It's a good story. And I'm learning something important about you. I like that."

Donna felt herself blush. "Well, after that, I realized how selfish I had been. I apologized to Odell, and I vowed to somehow make it up to him. I think that's part of why I started the White Students Against Racism chapter at Lakeside. I want things to change, and now I understand that it has to start with me. I know that if I make my stepdad proud, my real dad will be proud, too."

"Odell sounds like a real solid guy," Chuck said.

Donna smiled. "He really is," she said. "I wish it hadn't taken me so long to figure that out. But I've realized that my need to reach out to a black guy is due, in part, to my need to reach out to Odell. I'd never really made that connection before."

"So," Chuck said, his voice gentle, "you liked me because I remind you of your stepdad? Or was there more to it?"

Donna's smile turned into a wide grin. "I think there was a little more to it than that," she said.

"So, you think maybe we could start over?"

Donna nodded, and Chuck extended his hand. "My name is Chuck Johnson," he said, "and I was wondering if you would like to take a walk with me?"

Donna returned his handshake. "I'm Donna Sullivan, and I'd like that."

A few minutes later, they made their way along the lake trail. They found a quiet spot along the bank, separated from the rest of the retreat center by a thick tangle of trees. As they sat, Donna rested her head on Chuck's shoulder.

"We're missing lunch, you know," she said.

"That's all right. I'd rather spend some time alone with you."

"Honestly? You're not just saying that?"

"Hey, we're starting over, remember? After what you shared with me, I'd better be honest."

"It's hard isn't it?" Donna asked.

"I was hoping you hadn't noticed," he grinned.

Donna smacked him on the arm.

"Kidding!" he said. "What do you mean?"

"The whole black and white thing. It just gets in the way of everything. I mean, I really do think you're a nice guy. It's that simple, but somehow it gets complicated."

"I hear you. I worry my dogs will ride me if I don't try to jump your bones. I worry the sisters will come down on me with a world of hurt if I do get with you. Somehow the fact that I like talking to you and being with you gets lost in all of that."

"Do you think we'll ever learn to just 'be'?" Donna asked.

"I hope so. I don't know when I've been able to talk to anyone like this."

Chuck leaned close. Their lips touched softly at first, and then more intensely. In the distance, the retreat bell clanged, letting everyone know the next session was about to start.

"Saved by the bell," Chuck sighed, and then pulled her closer for a hug. "Can I see you later?"

She bit playfully on his lower lip. "I'd like that."

## CHAPTER TWENTY TWO

After lunch, the group reassembled in the Great Hall. "We need solutions for the problems we discussed at our last session," Dr. Oliver said. "We need to know where we go from here. Let's divide up into four groups again. Try to choose different ones from before, and we'll do some more brainstorming, okay?"

After about thirty minutes, Dr. Oliver asked to hear some of their ideas.

"Communication," Donna said, with a smile in Chuck's direction. "We need to learn to talk to one another as equals and to really listen to one another. We need to encourage others to be assertive and to express how they feel. That will help counteract a lot of the stereotyping."

"When it comes to actual harassment, like the cross burning, we need to have a racial harassment policy in place, just like we have for sexual harassment," Lori offered.

"Good," Dr. Oliver said. "What about faculty treating students differently because of their race?"

"The university should sponsor cultural sensitivity trainings, including a retreat like this for faculty members," Mark answered. "We could also talk to the administration about doing more to encourage minority applicants for staff openings. The only problem with that is the best person qualified for the job should be the one who gets it. If they hire someone based solely on their racial status, rather than their qualifications, then that's reverse discrimination. The ones who will suffer in the long run are us students."

"Qualified minority candidates are out there, it's just a matter of finding them," Bruce said.

"Why is it that the only time we use the word qualified, it is to refer to minority candidates?" Kwame asked. "Are there no mediocre white people? The problem with affirmative action is that it maintains white supremacy by putting the burden of proof on people of color, as if we're the only ones who could be unqualified." When Kwame sat back, Jamal leaned over and gave him a high five.

"Perhaps it also keeps us from uniting and asking why there can't be jobs for everyone who wants to work, or educational opportunities for everyone who wants to attend college," Dr. Oliver pointed out. "We spend our time fighting against each other for a piece of the pie, instead of working to expand it."

"I never thought of it quite that way," said Lori. "I think we just learned something. I know I did."

The discussion continued, as students offered other suggestions to encourage more social interaction between the races.

"We could have a mini cultural retreat during freshman orientation every year," Marjorie said, "and then student mentors could be chosen to help non-majority students find their niche."

Other suggestions included sponsoring cultural fun nights, ethnic meals, theme dances and debates on cultural issues.

"That's all well and good," Ashante pointed out, "but it's also a bit idealistic. Don't you think the students who will attend a cultural fun night are the ones who are already open minded? How will you make the bigoted students attend? After all, those are the ones you really need to reach."

"I don't think anything will change the hardcore bigots. They're just plain ignorant," another student responded.

"Are there ways of educating them?" Oliver asked.

"There could be curriculum requirements so everyone has to take a course on other cultures," Donna suggested. "We already have history requirements, but the focus is white people's history, with other races thrown in as an afterthought."

"So what, in order to get my degree, I'm going to have to take a class on every culture out there? Get real!" Stu said.

"There are no easy answers," Oliver agreed. "Just a lot of tough questions. The important thing is that you're all thinking about those questions now. It's a start."

The discussion continued at a lively pace until three-thirty, when Dr. Oliver called a halt.

"It's too beautiful of a day to spend any more of it inside," he said. "You have two and a half hours of free time. I'd like for you to continue your discussions and remember how half of your free time is to be spent."

Chuck and Donna looked at each other and grinned.

"But wait," Jamal said. He turned to Dan, sitting at the back of the room. "Dan, I heard you wanted to speak to us," Jamal asked.

Dan glanced around nervously. "I do—I mean, I will, first thing tomorrow morning."

"Alright, that's settled," Dr. Oliver said. "I'll see everyone at supper."

***

Gloria was glad to escape the confines of the Great Hall. She let Ashante and Lori go on without her and wandered down to the lake, in search of a quiet place to think. A small bench sat amid the underbrush, close enough to the water's edge that Gloria could smell the slight tang of lake water and feel the light breeze against her cheeks. If someone had told her at the start of the semester that this is where she'd be, she would've called them crazy. It felt like blinders had fallen from her eyes; and though she knew she'd grown stronger and more certain since what happened on their lawn, she also felt raw and worn out. What would life be like when they went back to campus? Would she always be defining herself as *G.W. Before* and *G.W. After*?

Gloria was so lost in thought that she didn't notice Jamal until he sat down beside her. "Did you forget your buddy?" he asked.

"What? Oh, right, the buddy system. I don't know, I just needed to get away, I guess. This 'woman with a cause' stuff is running me ragged." Gloria gave him a searching look. "How do you do it, Jamal? How do you stay so dedicated? I've only been involved with all this for a few weeks, and I'm worn out. I want to do my part to make a difference, but another part of me just wishes all of this had never happened so I could just go back to being the plain, old G.W. from before."

Jamal shook his head, but instead of the fired-up tone Gloria had grown used to, his words were matter-of-fact and subdued. "Wishing all of this away is a waste of time," he told her. "You always were a part of it; you just weren't an active player. Now you're in the game, and nothing can change that."

"I know, but don't you ever get tired of fighting? I doubt we'll win this in our lifetime, you know. I suppose you think I'm shallow and selfish for wishing my old life back."

"No, I don't think that," Jamal said, quietly. "To tell you the truth, I often feel the same way. I don't enjoy being angry all the time. The problems we face as a race tear at my guts, day in and day out."

"Then why do you do it?"

Jamal sighed, and he gave Gloria a slight, sad smile. "It's how I was raised," he said. "My father is a minister. He's a leader in the civil rights movement in our hometown. He always had big goals for me as a spokesperson for our people. He believes the key lies in politics, so he's grooming me as the next 'voice in the wilderness.' He was a follower of Malcolm X. That's where I got the nickname, Little Malcolm."

"Is that what you want to do—go into politics?"

"I guess so. I never really gave much thought to anything else. It's real important to me to make my father proud. My older brother, Bobby, was going to be a minister, just like our dad. Pops was so proud of him."

"Was? What happened?"

Jamal glanced out across the lake; in the distance Gloria could hear the shouts and laughter of other students goofing around. Jamal was quiet for so long that Gloria worried she'd offended him by asking such a personal question. But then she felt his shoulders sag back against the park bench as he began to speak.

"He was smoked three years ago," Jamal said. "He got caught up in the drug scene. The devil's dick—I'm sorry, the crack pipe—had him strung out near the end." Jamal was speaking softly, his voice laced with bitterness. "He was in the wrong place at the wrong time, trying to cop, and a gang banger shot him."

"That's terrible!" Gloria said. "It must have devastated your family."

"My father hasn't been the same since. The life drained right out of him when Bobby died. I think he blames himself for staying in that neighborhood."

"So now there's even more pressure on you to live up to your father's expectations."

"Don't get me wrong," Jamal said. "I really believe in what I'm doing. I'm not just acting as a mouthpiece for my father. But there is added pressure on me now that Bobby's gone. My father was so happy when I got accepted to Lakeside. It was the first time I had seen him smile in months."

"What about your mother?"

"She died in a car accident when I was twelve. It's been hard without her, but I'm glad she wasn't there to see what happened to Bobby. I still remember her preaching at us to avoid drugs at all costs. It would have crushed her to see him going down that road."

Gloria heard the sadness in his voice, and she fought the urge to reach for his hand. "How do you deal with all of it?" she asked softly. "I guess I've lived a pretty sheltered life. Some cops harassed my little brother a while ago, but other than that and the cross burning, nothing serious has happened to my family. It's strange, but when I hear things like what you've been through, I feel kind of guilty that I've had it so easy."

"Don't apologize because you've had a good life so far. After all, that's what we're fighting for, for all of our people."

A comfortable silence stretched between them as they gazed out over the lake. Laughter carried across the water. A bunch of students were canoeing, while others swam and splashed off a narrow sandbar.

Gloria glanced up at Jamal and broke the silence. "Can I ask you something?" she said.

"Sure."

"Has something changed? You seem calmer or something. I mean, you usually act like you're ready to explode, like the way you went off on Bruce this morning. But now you seem like you've let go of some of that."

Jamal gave a slight frown, and Gloria could tell he was thinking of the best way to answer her. "I didn't see much value in this retreat at first," he finally said. "But now I realize that whether we like it or not, it's forcing us to talk to people we otherwise wouldn't give the time of day to. I guess you could say it has opened my eyes a bit."

"Like how?"

"Well, take Bruce for instance. I thought he was a sellout just like so many other white people I've met, but it ends up he's been helping us all along."

"What do you mean?"

"He's been digging around. He confronted me this morning just so he could give me a heads up on what he's found."

"Really? What's he got?"

"Well, he pulled my coattail on Rush and Stu."

"He thinks they did it? Does he know anything for sure?"

"Not enough to nail them, but we're on the right track. He's also a personal friend of Steve Walsh, the guy from the newspaper—so that explains why Steve has been so supportive."

"That's good news for once. What about Dan? Did Bruce say anything about him?" Gloria asked.

"Not to me, why?"

"Dan apologized to me during the group session last night. I tried talking to him last night, but Stu showed up and dragged him away. Dr. Oliver told me Dan wants to tell the whole group something. He really seems upset. I was thinking maybe he was the one who burned the cross, but he really doesn't seem the type."

"Yeah, but Rush and Stu sure do," Jamal said. "What I can't figure out is why they would single out you and Ashante? I have the feeling we're missing something. Do you think Oliver is right? Have we been blinded by all the racist rhetoric and missed what's really going on?"

"I've been asking myself the same thing. The cross was such a shock, I couldn't really see beyond it. Rush and Stu are everything I expect when it comes to rednecks, but Dan doesn't fit the mold. He's really torn up about something, but if he's involved, I'd have to think he was forced into it."

"How 'bout we go talk to Dr. Oliver and pick his brain some more? But before we do, there's something I've been dying to do." Jamal leaned over and gave Gloria a lingering, affectionate hug. "I hope you don't mind," he said softly, as they parted.

Gloria suppressed a smile. "I'm more surprised than anything else," she said. "I didn't think you cared."

"I've been a blind fool when it comes to you," Jamal said, "but not any longer." As they stood up, Jamal reached over and took her hand.

On their way back to the Great Hall, they passed Chuck and Donna on the trail.

"Hey there," Jamal said, "where are you two headed?"

"Nature hike," Chuck said, grinning. Donna's face flushed, but she grinned, too, as Chuck pulled her on into the woods.

Jamal and Gloria passed more students along their way and noticed that everyone seemed to be more comfortable. A flag football game was underway, girls against guys. Ashante was showing several girls how to braid their hair into a cornrow.

"People are really starting to talk to each other, aren't they?" Gloria said. "I never would have thought there'd be such a difference in this short amount of time."

"Me, neither," Jamal agreed. "I notice it's not all just talking, either." He nodded at several couples lounging beneath the trees. "And Chuck and Donna. 'Nature hike,' my ass!"

Gloria laughed. "Does it bother you?" she said.

"What, doin' the wild thing?"

Gloria blushed. "That's not what I meant. I mean, do you have a problem with interracial couples?"

"I'm not into that, myself. The way I look at it, there are enough fine black sisters to keep a brother busy without ever having to look elsewhere. What about you? Most of the sisters I know take it pretty personally when some white chick lays claim to a black dude."

"It's not an issue for me," Gloria said. "I don't tell anyone who they can or cannot love, and hopefully they'll do the same for me. The only issue I have is when a brother or sister only exclusively dates outside their race. Then it feels personal, because I feel they're giving up on all of us—on our culture—and that hurts."

As they passed the courts, an errant volleyball came sailing at them and stopped their conversation. Startled, they looked up to find Dr. Oliver and the other staff in the midst of a volleyball game. Dr. Oliver missed an easy spike, tumbled to the ground, and lay there laughing at himself. Gloria and Jamal watched as he accepted a hand up from Ms. Jones.

"Thanks," Dr. Oliver told her.

"Anytime," Ms. Jones replied.

"I guess volleyball isn't my sport," Oliver said, brushing the sand from his clothing.

"Maybe you'd like to sit this next game out with me," Ms. Jones said. "That would give us a chance to get to know each other better."

Gloria glanced up at Jamal and shot him a surprised look.

To his surprise, Oliver realized she was flirting with him. He was taken aback by his own stirring interest. He hadn't even thought about another woman since Sarah's death and he felt a bit uneasy. "Actually, I promised I'd help out with the meal preparations," Dr. Oliver said. "I make a mean cornbread."

"Oh, I see," Ms. Jones said, and Gloria could hear the disappointment in her voice.

"Would you like to join me, Ms. Jones?" Dr. Oliver asked.

Ms. Jones smiled. "You can call me Andrea," she said, "and yes, I would."

"Call me Wendell, then," he stammered.

As they turned and walked toward the mess hall, Gloria and Jamal turned to stare at one another. "Wow," Gloria said. "I think we'll have to wait until after dinner to talk to him."

"Yep, the man is gettin' busy," Jamal agreed.

## CHAPTER TWENTY THREE

The free time spent in the fresh air gave everyone an appetite, so the dining hall filled up early. Dr. Oliver stood at the front of the room. "Now, some of you may have had soul food before," he said. "The phrase was popularized in the 1960s, but the origins of this cuisine can be traced back to Africa, Native American cultures, and even parts of Europe."

Several of the students exchanged surprised looks.

"That's right," Dr. Oliver said. "You see, this history of soul food is directly intertwined with the history of the slave experience. They say you can learn a lot about a culture based on its food. Well, you can learn a lot about the history of black people in America based solely on what's on that table. Let's get to it!"

With that, Dr. Oliver invited the cooks to step forward and introduce each dish: fried chicken, collard greens, country mashed potatoes smothered in onion gravy, buttered rice, black-eyed peas, candied yams, and hot skillet cornbread. As the cooks explained how each item was prepared, Dr. Oliver interjected with facts and historical details.

Okra and rice, he told them, came to the United States from West Africa, through the trans-Atlantic slave trade. And cornbread and grits were inspired by maize and hominy, popular to Native American tribes across the southern U.S., like the Cherokee and the Creek.

As a cook unveiled a steaming dish of collard greens, Dr. Oliver explained how plantation owners would often feed their enslaved workers scraps left over from the kitchen—the tops of turnips and dandelions, for example. "Those were the first 'greens'," Dr. Oliver told them.

Instead of setting up a buffet line, the cooks carried large serving plates to each table. "We're going to eat 'family style' tonight," Dr. Oliver explained. "At the center of African American foodways is the concept of sharing and togetherness. We don't just eat to sustain ourselves; we eat as a way to be together, and to share what we have."

The students dug in, passing the plates around each table. Some students were hesitant about trying the greens, but they discovered they actually enjoyed the flavor. After dinner, the cooks brought out dishes of sweet potato pie and bowls of ice cream.

"Wow," Lori said, as the meal wrapped up. "I haven't been this full in ages. That was amazing!"

Mark leaned back in his chair and rubbed his stomach with both hands. "I never really thought about the stories behind my dinner," he said.

Dr. Oliver nodded. "Every family and every culture has its own foodways," he said. "For example, Mr. Polaski, I bet your Polish grandmother could make her own version of this feast, no?"

Chris grinned. "She sure could," he said.

"Food is a uniter," Dr. Oliver said. "We all need to eat!"

"True," said Lori, "though I probably don't need to eat again anytime soon!"

The women had clean-up duty. Judith Hall, Ashante's bunkmate, was clearing glasses from a table when one of them shattered in her hand.

"Yikes!" she yelped, as blood trickled down her palm.

Ashante grabbed a clean dishrag and ran over. "Here," she said, "let me see it."

Ashante took Judith's hand and cradled it, applying just enough pressure with the rag. "I don't think you'll need stitches," she told Judith. "Just relax. It'll be okay."

"Thanks," Judith said, some of the color returning to her face.

Ashante smiled. "Don't mention it."

"Hey, Ashante," Judith said, once the bleeding stopped. "I wanted to ask if you and Gloria ever thought about pledging a sorority. I know there aren't any black sororities on campus, but have you thought about Pi Beta Phi? I think we'd be lucky to have you."

Ashante looked startled. "Really? I always heard there was an unwritten rule against black women joining. I went to a recruiting social during Rush Week once. I don't remember which one, but they obviously weren't expecting someone of my, uh, skin tone. You could have heard a pin drop when I walked in. I gulped down some punch and headed for the door, all the while pretending not to notice how relieved they were to see me go!"

"Well, some of us are trying to change that," Judith said. "If you're brave enough to give it another go, I'm brave enough to put in a good word for you. What do you think?"

"I'll check with G.W. Thanks for the offer," Ashante said.

***

After they finished cleaning up, Gloria and Ashante joined Jamal, Kwame and Bruce outside the Dining Hall. Chuck and Donna were already outside enjoying each other's company. The group lingered there for a few minutes, making small talk, happy and full from the evening's meal. But as the retreat bell rang, summoning everyone down to the bonfire site, Gloria felt a sudden wave of panic. The scent of smoke wafted in their direction. She glanced toward the flames flickering in the distance, and her stomach lurched. Dozens of students swarmed around them, chatting and laughing as they walked down the path toward the fire. But Gloria didn't move.

"I'm not sure I can do this," she said. She looked at Jamal, aware of the alarm in her voice. "I'm not sure I'm ready."

Ashante nodded and moved to stand next to Gloria. "I feel like I've finally stopped having nightmares," Ashante said. "Why did they do this? What was Dr. Oliver thinking?"

Most of the other students had already made their way to the bonfire site; Gloria and her friends stood there alone. It had grown dark, and she could see the orange-white glow through the trees; she wasn't sure, but she imagined she could even hear the sound of the wood burning, breaking off, and hitting the ground with a hiss. The thought of it made her shiver.

"I can't do it," Gloria finally said, shaken but determined.

"Wait a second," Jamal said. "You two have been facing your fears for the past month. You refused to let them run you out of your house. You've spoken up at rallies. You've shown all the rest of us what real courage is. Don't let this bonfire stop you now."

Gloria gave a weak smile. "I appreciate what you're saying. But the thought of fire makes me nauseous. I'm not sure I can sit through an entire evening in front of one."

"I agree with Jamal on this one," Bruce said. "Look, Gloria, you've inspired us. You've got every student on this retreat totally behind you."

"Exactly," Kwame said, "we got your back. It won't be like last time—it won't be anything like that. Besides—this is the first chance that we've had for some fun on this retreat! Even Malcolm and Martin had some fun every now and then."

Chuck and Donna nodded their support.

Gloria took a deep breath. She didn't like the idea of being frightened after all she and Ashante had been through. She liked to think of herself as stronger than that now. "Alright," she said. She glanced at her housemate. "If Ashante is willing to go, I'll go, too."

Before she could say anything, Kwame ran over to Ashante, turned his back to her and bent over, "Piggy back ride to the bonfire! Jump on!" he shouted.

Ashante laughed. "Alright, alright," she said. "Let's do it."

They made their way down the trail, winding away from the Dining Hall. About halfway to the bonfire site, they saw a smaller fire burning off to the side of the path.

Gloria felt herself stiffen. "What's that?" she said.

The group stopped and looked: The fire was small and contained; it looked like it was coming from an old bucket. A gust of wind blew across the path, and with it came a sharp, acrid odor.

"Do you smell that?" Ashante cried. "It's the same smell as—."

"The cross," Gloria finished, as her stomach flipped upside down.

"Are you sure it's the same," Bruce asked.

Chuck shook his head. "It's the same, man. After I carried the remains of the cross away, I had that smell on me for days."

"Trust me," Gloria said. "That smell was burned into my nightmares."

They were standing at the edge of the path, the small fire just a few feet away. The light from the Dining Hall barely reached this far. Gloria felt the movement more than she saw it—a rustling in the bushes off to the left. "Who's there?" she cried out.

Suddenly there was a hissing sound, and they realized the small fire had been extinguished. Gloria squinted; she thought she saw a figure running off in the opposite direction, but it was too dark for her to be sure.

"What the hell is going on?" Jamal demanded. He started to rush in the direction of the smoldering bucket, but Bruce grabbed his arm.

"I think that was Dan," he said.

"What are you talking about?" Gloria said.

"Whoever it was that just put out that fire—I think I recognized him."

"But why?" Ashante said. "Why would he do that? Light a fire like that, and then run off?"

Gloria felt the panic begin to creep back in. "It was almost like he was waiting for us," she said.

"Maybe he was trying to send a message," Kwame said.

Gloria shook her head. "No," she said. "Not a message—a clue. I think he was trying to leave us a clue."

Jamal turned to Gloria and Ashante. "You okay?" he asked. "You want to turn back?"

Gloria and Ashante glanced at each other. "Actually," Gloria said, "I think it might be best if we stick together."

"You sure?" Jamal said.

"Definitely," Gloria said. "Besides, tomorrow morning Dan's going to speak to all of us, right? I hope we'll get some answers then."

Jamal smiled. "Let's go, then," he said. "If we hurry, we'll catch the start of the show."

They approached the clearing around the bonfire just as Dr. Oliver was giving his official welcome. "Welcome to our impromptu talent show," he was saying. "This is your chance to wow your peers, people! The rules are simple," Dr. Oliver said. "Have fun, don't be shy, and remember—we're not here to be the best, we're here to enjoy ourselves. So, who's up first?"

Darryl Jefferson, a black freshman, and two of his friends jumped up to the center of the circle. The flickering light of the bonfire acted as a spotlight, as the trio managed to pull off a surprisingly professional rap song.

Everyone else hollered and clapped as Darryl and his friends sat down, but Gloria sat quietly, trying her best to breath in as little air as possible. Her eyes stung, and her pulse raced and she kept telling herself to relax. Ashante reached over and held her hand.

Next up, Chris and Bruce decided to try their hands at rapping, as well. By the time the song was through, the entire crowd was doubled over in laughter. Even Gloria and Ashante couldn't hold back.

Next, Mark led a group of students in the latest country line dance. He even managed to coax Jamal into trying it. Jamal was a good sport, but he was relieved to kick the music over to a hip-hop beat. He showed Gloria the latest in bump-and-grind, accompanied by whistles from the onlookers.

Dr. Oliver led the students in what he called the St. Louis Super Soul Charge. It was sort of like a soul train line but everyone had to pair up. It was a wild, sexy dance, and the students loved it. Ms. Jones ended up as Oliver's partner, which disconcerted and intrigued him at the same time. Gloria paired with Jamal while Kwame danced with Ashante. For the first time that night they were having fun, and they allowed themselves to enjoy the moment.

Donna and Chuck drew more laughs with their attempt at a duet; they forgot most of the words and eventually ended up just whistling and humming. Judith and Lori convinced Ashante and Gloria to join them in singing an old Supremes song as the students cheered and egged them on, while Kwame brought down the house with his off-key rendition of James Brown's *I Feel Good*.

Even the staff members got into the act, teaming up in a barbershop quartet with amazingly good results.

As the talent show ended, Dr. Oliver allowed the evening to naturally wind down. Some students stayed to enjoy the bonfire, while others drifted away in small groups or paired off in couples.

Without drawing any attention from the other students, Dr. Oliver quietly tapped on the shoulders of Gloria, Ashante, Jamal and Bruce, and motioned for them to follow him inside, to the Great Hall.

They pulled a few chairs into a small circle, and after they settled in, Dr. Oliver turned to Gloria.

"Have you had a chance to talk with Dan yet?" he asked her.

Gloria shook her head. "I tried to, last night, but Stu dragged him away before he could say anything. "But tonight I think he tried to give us a clue."

"What do you mean," Dr. Oliver asked.

They quickly filled him in on the burning bucket and Dan's dashing away.

"It was the same awful chemical smell from the cross burning," Ashante said.

"Gloria thought he was waiting for us," Jamal added.

"Very interesting," Dr. Oliver said. "I tried talking with him earlier today, but he said he needed more time to collect his thoughts. I was hoping I could catch up with him this evening; but what you all have just told me may explain why I haven't seen him tonight—or Stu or Rush, for that matter."

"Speaking of those two," Jamal said, "Bruce has some new information. Bruce, tell Dr. Oliver and Ashante what you told me—I've already filled Gloria in."

After Bruce shared his suspicions, Dr. Oliver reached into his pocket without a word and pulled out a small tape recorder.

"I have something to share with all of you," he said. "I think you'll find it most interesting. It's a phone call Dean Severson placed to President Horning from my cabin when you came to see me that day, Gloria."

Dr. Oliver pressed *play*. They listened intently as Severson admitted to orchestrating the theft of Ashante's tape and alluded to something even more sinister—the outright cover-up of the cross burning.

As the tape rolled to a stop, they sat back in their chairs, momentarily silent, caught somewhere between disbelief and anger.

"Looks like you were right, Bruce," Ashante finally said. "They're clearly covering for someone."

"Two someones," Gloria said, recalling Severson's slip-up on the plane.

"But which two?" Bruce said. "Rush and Stu? How do we find out for sure?"

"Dr. Oliver," Gloria asked, "why didn't you tell us about this tape before?"

"I didn't want to take it out of context," he said. "I was waiting for more of a connection. Bruce's suspicions might be the tie-in."

"So you think it was Rush and Stu?" Gloria said.

Dr. Oliver seemed to weigh his words carefully. "I think it's worth looking into," he told them.

"But something doesn't make sense," Gloria said. "How does Dan fit into all of this? From what I gather, he doesn't have rich parents that could pay off the university to cover for him. I found out he's not even in the Sigma frat. He just hangs out with Rush and Stu, but they don't exactly seem to be best friends, by any means."

"Yeah, but I'm sure he started that fire tonight," Bruce said.

"If he did," Gloria said, "he used the same chemicals that smelled up our yard. Either that was an awfully dirty joke, or it was his way of finally telling the truth."

"Well, he obviously knows something," Jamal said. "Why else would he apologize to Gloria and say he needs to talk to the whole group? Maybe Stu dragged him away from Gloria to keep him from talking. Who knows? I think we should go find Dan and see what he has to say."

Dr. Oliver stood up, signaling their covert meeting was nearing its end. "I know this is a lot to ask all of you—especially you, Gloria and Ashante—but please let it go for now," Dr. Oliver said. "Give Dan some time. Let me try to talk to him again in the morning."

Gloria and Ashante looked disappointed, but Jamal quickly rose to his feet. "All right, sir. We'll follow your lead," he said, extending his hand toward Dr. Oliver. "I have to admit, you've been taking care of business."

"Thank you, Jamal," Dr. Oliver replied. "That means a lot. Well, folks, let's call it a night. Make sure you're all here tomorrow morning. I'm going to need each of you if we're to get to the bottom of this."

As the students headed for the door, Dr. Oliver remained behind to prepare for the next day's activities.

"Heavy stuff," Bruce said once they'd stepped outside. A few students remained by the fire, which was nothing more than a pile of orange embers. They could hear murmurs and light laughter in the darkness.

"Yeah, but it's a good thing we're on to them," Ashante said.

"I guess so," Gloria said. "I guess I'd hoped the cover-up wasn't actually true. Even after all this, that tape was hard to listen to. I still had a tiny sliver of hope that Severson and Horning were capable of doing the right thing."

Ashante shook her head and let out a wry laugh. "Ever the optimist, aren't you, G.W.," she said.

Before Gloria could respond, Jamal came to her defense. "It's not bad to have faith in people," he said. The rest of the group looked at him in surprise.

"Did I hear you right?" Bruce asked, in mock-alarm. "Who are you, and what'd you do with Jamal Washington?"

"All I'm saying is, power corrupts. It's doesn't mean the person underneath is necessarily evil. I don't know Severson and Horning personally—but I know corruption when I see it."

"I can't say I disagree with you," Bruce said, "I'm just surprised to hear you say it."

Jamal smiled. "What can I say? I'm the son of a preacher. My dad believed everyone, deep down, was capable of some kind of goodness. I can't help it if some of that rubbed off."

"Fair enough," Bruce said, as the four of them burst out laughing.

Ashante and Bruce wandered back to their cabins, leaving Gloria and Jamal to themselves.

"You tired?" Jamal asked her.

"Not really. I feel kind of agitated, to tell you the truth."

"Well, walk with me then," he said. Jamal took her hand, and they wandered back down to the lake. They lingered on the park bench in silence for a while, enjoying the quiet night air and the beauty of the moonlight reflecting off the water. After a while, Jamal draped his arm over Gloria's shoulder.

"You're awfully quiet," she said. "What are you thinking about?"

"Actually, for the first time since all this, happened my mind is on something other than nailing those bastards," Jamal said.

"Really? What's that?"

"I was wondering what you're doing here with me. Most women think I'm too obsessed with the cause. Once they get to know me, they hit the ground running."

Gloria rested her head against Jamal's shoulder. "I think you take on way too much," she said. "You try to save the world all on your own, but it doesn't make me want to run. It makes me want to help. When I'm with you, I feel like I can make a difference."

Jamal shifted and turned so that they sat face-to-face. He noticed the way her smooth skin offset her warm, almond eyes, and the way her dark hair fell softly around her face. Truly, she was chocolate thunder.

"So what about you?" Gloria asked softly. "What are you doing here with me?"

"I'm not really sure," Jamal said candidly, still gazing at her as if for the first time. "I just know I feel a little more hopeful about everything—even the future—when I'm with you."

They stared at each other for a few moments, and then Jamal gently removed her glasses. He leaned forward and pressed his lips softly to hers. Gloria closed her eyes and returned the kiss, feeling her knees start to tremble. It was several moments before they parted. Jamal was the first one to speak.

"That was some deep sugar," he said, his voice thick with wonder.

"I haven't had much practice," Gloria said.

"A fine sister like you? You must have had tons of dates."

"Not really. In fact, until all this happened with the cross and everything, I spent most of my Saturday nights at home."

"I find that hard to believe." Jamal said. "What about in high school?"

Gloria shook her head with a grimace. "I didn't have time for any of that. I'm the first one in my family to make it to college, and it wasn't easy getting here. I had to study my butt off every night. That's not the way to get dates. Besides, look at me. I'm not exactly a cover girl."

"Please!" Jamal said. "I think you're a knockout."

"You probably drop that line on all the sisters."

"To be honest, I don't remember the last time I thought about dropping a line on anyone. There've been too many other things going on. Besides, I've never been all that smooth when it comes to the ladies. Look how long it took for me to open my eyes to you."

"I admit I was beginning to wonder," Gloria teased.

"So, I'm slow," he said, leaning forward to kiss her again. "Seriously, G.W., I think you're really something. I haven't met anyone like you since..."

"Since when?"

"Ah, nothing."

"No, go on. An old girlfriend?"

Jamal nodded. "Lucretia. We dated for almost three years in high school."

"What happened?"

"We were really serious—we even talked about getting married. Then Bobby died, and I got accepted at Lakeside. I got busy with school, and I was so worried about helping my father deal with what happened to Bobby, that I got distracted. Lucretia decided to go to college closer to home. She thought it would be better if we put things on hold until I had a chance to work through Bobby's death.

"In retrospect I think even before Bobby's death, she wasn't sure we would end up in the same place. We tried the long distance thing for a while, but it was a lot tougher than either one of us thought.

"Last year when I went home for spring break, she told me she'd fallen in love with my best friend, Ronald. He had time for her, she told me, and his priorities were more in line with hers. She never truly understood my passion for civil rights. She thought it was a waste of time. She and Ronald got married this past summer."

"I'm sorry," Gloria said, squeezing his hand. "I always seem to drag up your painful memories, don't I?"

"It's not that big of a deal anymore. We weren't meant to be together. I could never have made it work with someone so indifferent to her race."

"Still, it had to be tough."

"That was then," Jamal said. "I'd rather concentrate on what's here now—or, I should say, who's here now."

He smiled and pulled her close to him again. Gloria welcomed his soft kisses. When his hand caressed her breast, though, she pulled away.

"Someone might be watching," she said, glancing around.

"You want to go somewhere?"

Gloria fidgeted uncomfortably.

"What's wrong?" he said.

"I just—I guess I just want to go slow," Gloria said, her face flushing. "When I said I wasn't very experienced, I meant it. I've never, well, you know."

"You mean you're a virgin?" Jamal asked, his eyes widening. "I didn't know there were any of those left!"

Gloria pulled away from him and crossed her arms protectively. "Yeah, well, I am. So I guess this is where you take off running, right?"

"Why would I do that?"

"Because there are few things scarier to a guy than a virgin, right? Guys assume that if you're a virgin, you're desperate and just waiting to trap them. Most of them panic and run. Well, I'm not desperate and I'm not looking to trap anyone. I just happen to think it's worth waiting for the right person. Go ahead and laugh."

"Do you see me laughing?" Jamal reached for her hand. "I was just surprised. I certainly don't think you're desperate. I think you're probably the classiest woman I've ever known. My mother would have loved you."

"Don't say things like that unless you mean it."

Jamal tipped her chin up and looked into her eyes. "Man, any brother who ran from you had to be crazy," Jamal told her. "I'm not going anywhere."

He felt her relax against him.

"Okay?" he said.

Gloria nodded. "Okay."

"I don't mind if we take this slow, G.W. How's that sound?"

"That sounds perfect," she said, "as long as it's not *too* slow!"

## CHAPTER TWENTY FOUR

The next morning dawned cloudy and wet. It was the final day of the retreat, and suspense hung in the air. As they gathered their things and began to move toward the Great Hall for the morning's first session, Gloria ran up to find Jamal and Bruce. "We have a problem," she told them. "Look around—Dan isn't here. He never came to breakfast."

"Don't worry," Jamal said, scanning the room. "He probably just slept in."

"Yeah, or he might've gotten sick," Bruce said. "Chris Polaski was up all night with some nasty bug. Said he'd try to make it to the session later on. It's possible there's something going around."

The retreat bell clanged, and all around them students hurried to find their seats. "I guess we'll just have to wait and see," Gloria said, an uneasy feeling settling in her stomach.

The morning session had been set aside for answering the question, *Where do we go from here?* Dr. Oliver told them that this was the only true lecture he was going to deliver at the retreat. "It's intended to challenge your mind," he said, "while engaging your spirit."

"Nap time," said Stu, as other students grumbled, as well. But their apathy quickly turned to excitement when Dr. Oliver broke into the old Negro spiritual, *Let My People Go.* All around the room, students watched and listened with awe. "Beautiful, just beautiful," Ashante said. Gloria was so taken by the sound of Dr. Oliver's voice that she temporarily forgot about Dan.

Next, Dr. Oliver asked the students to close their eyes and go back in time with him to the slave-holding South. He explained why he selected that particular song. He lectured on the black codes that were written as state and federal laws to suppress black people. He talked about how every institution in the nation, from the courts to the church, was used to uphold slavery.

He wrote down five key topics for discussion and engaged students on each one: *The Legacy of Slavery; Institutional Racism, Then and Now; White Privilege; Ways to Heal Racial Animosity; and Coalition Building.* He connected the past and the present in ways students had never heard before. Even Jamal was enraptured.

Dr. Oliver described how blacks and whites had worked together to launch the Underground Railroad and fight for emancipation. This lesson of racial cooperation was what he wanted them to remember—especially when they returned to campus.

When he finished, the students erupted in emotional applause. "That was the most eloquent presentation I have ever heard," Donna said. Almost everyone in the room nodded in agreement.

Gloria raised her hand. "Dr. Oliver," she said, "would you mind standing in the middle of the circle and let us whisper in your ear what your lecture meant to us individually?"

Dr. Oliver was deeply moved as he made his way to the center of the circle.

"Now, close your eyes," Ashante instructed.

Gloria had just stepped up to hug him when the side door burst open and Chris Polaski rushed in.

"Hurry! He's hung himself!" Chris shouted. "Dr. Oliver! Hurry!"

Shouts and questions broke the stunned silence as the students surged toward the door. Dr. Oliver and Gloria got there first and rushed out after Chris. But once they left, Professor Reese blocked the door and firmly requested that the rest of the students remain in their seats.

The room erupted in a buzz of questions.

"What's going on?"

"Who hung himself?"

"Shouldn't somebody call the police?"

The faculty members didn't have any answers. The minutes crawled by as the students waited.

Finally, Dr. Oliver returned. He ignored the students' anxious pleas and quietly conferred with the faculty members at the front of the room. Then he turned and faced the crowd.

"There has been an unfortunate incident," Dr. Oliver told the students. "I am very sorry to tell you this, but Dan Trent has been injured."

"Is he dead?" someone shouted from the back of the room.

"He's terribly shaken up, but he should recover," Dr. Oliver said. "In fact, as we speak, an ambulance is taking our friend to the hospital, where he will receive all the care he needs."

With that, Stu and Rush jumped from their chairs and bolted out the door. Professor Reese started to go after them, but Dr. Oliver shook his head and motioned instead for Bruce to follow them.

"See where they're headed, but don't do anything," Dr. Oliver told Bruce. "I'll send Professor Reese out in a few minutes."

The room erupted in noise once again, but Dr. Oliver waved his hand for silence. His voice was stern and somber. "In light of this incident, you are going to return to Lakeside earlier than expected. You are dismissed to go back to your cabins. Please pack your things immediately and return to the Great Hall. The bus will be here in one hour."

"But what about the rest of the program?" someone shouted.

"You'll continue some of the discussion on the bus trip back," Oliver said. "Due to the seriousness of the situation, it is best that we return you to the safety of your school. You have all made remarkable progress, even in the short time we've had. You're communicating with one another, which is the most important thing. As long as those channels are kept open, there's hope to solve any issue. I have faith you will do just that."

"But what's the deal with Dan?" someone called out. "What happened to him?"

"Your student body president will be hosting a campus-wide assembly tomorrow," Dr. Oliver said. "You will receive more details then. Unfortunately, we have no more time for questions. Let's get moving, people, back to your cabins."

As the students hurried for the door, Dr. Oliver motioned for Ashante and Jamal to stay behind.

"Is Dan really okay?" Ashante asked, once the room was clear.

"He's on his way to the hospital," Dr. Oliver said. "He should be fine other than some bruises. He asked Gloria to go with him. I think he's ready to make a full confession to her."

"Well, he'd better come clean," Jamal said. "I know the dude was upset, but it's still hard to believe he'd try to kill himself."

"Actually, Dan didn't hang himself," Oliver said.

Ashante and Jamal exchanged a startled look. "Then what happened?" she said. "Chris said he'd hung himself!"

"Apparently he had help."

"What do you mean?"

"Rush and Stu," Dr. Oliver said.

"Those fools hung him?" Jamal said.

"The cross burning had been weighing very heavy on him," Dr. Oliver told them. "He was at a breaking point. He told me he was on his way to admit what had happened to the whole group, but Rush and Stu waylaid him."

"And then they hung him," Ashante said, her voice heavy with shock.

"They tried to. They set it up to look like a suicide. With how jumpy Dan has been all weekend, I assume they figured no one would have trouble believing it. Luckily for Dan, his pals miscalculated. When they hung him from the shower stall, they didn't think about him standing on his tiptoes. He played dead long enough for them to believe it. When they left, he was able to put just enough slack in the rope to breathe. When Chris came in, Dan was afraid it was Rush and Stu coming back, so he pretended to be dead."

"Man, this is serious," Jamal said.

"Oh, before I forget—Ashante, Dan gave me your missing tape," Dr. Oliver said, handing her the cassette.

"My tape? How did he get it?"

"Apparently, he stole it from your purse. The important thing is, it doesn't appear to be damaged."

"I can clean it up as soon as I get back to Lakeside. I can't wait to hear what's on it."

"What will happen to those thugs?" Jamal asked.

"If my plan works, they'll be spending next semester at the State Pen," Dr. Oliver said. "I've asked Ms. Ford to call Dean Severson and have him send the campus police here to arrest them."

Bruce rushed back into the hall. "They're in Stu's cabin, Dr. Oliver. Professor Reese is keeping an eye on them."

"So, what did they do after they split out of here?" Jamal asked.

"Stu made a call on his cell phone. I hung back a little, but because he was literally shouting in the phone I could clearly hear what he said. I heard him say that 'all hell was breaking loose and that they had better get their asses in gear and fix things, or they'd be sorry'. That's almost a direct quote," Bruce said. "And guess who he was talking to?"

Jamal and Ashante spoke in unison. "Severson," they said.

"You got it," Bruce said. "At that point, he noticed me and hung up. Then Professor Reese came over and sent them to pack."

"I think things just got interesting," Dr. Oliver told them. "We have a chance to put all the pieces together. I've already given Gloria her instructions. Here's what I need each of you to do."

\*\*\*

Back at Lakeside, Severson rushed into Horning's office and slammed the door.

"The shit's hit the fan! I told those two idiots we'd take care of it, but they went and took matters into their own hands. Ms. Ford just called and asked me to send Officer Rodriquez. Damn it! What are we going to do?"

*** 

On the way to the hospital, Dan couldn't wait to talk to Gloria.

"I asked you to ride along because I need to come clean with you," he told her.

"Try not to talk," she said, patting his shoulder. "You can tell me later, after the doctors have looked at you."

"No, Gloria! My physical injuries will mend, but the guilt and shame won't go away until you and Ashante forgive me."

Gloria pulled her hand away. "Why did you do it?"

"I didn't burn the cross, but I know who did and why. I'm just as guilty as they are, because I participated in covering it up, and I stole the tape from Ashante's purse."

Gloria gasped. "You did that?" she said.

Dan nodded. "I didn't want to do it. I tried to tell you several times, but I couldn't bring myself to betray my sister."

"Your sister?"

"Yeah, she's deeply involved in all of this. I was going to tell you last night but Stu threatened me. I managed to send you a signal, though. Did you get it?"

"Loud and clear," Gloria said. "It brought back all the painful memories of the cross burning. What was that stuff?"

"Just some real cheap charcoal lighter fluid with a chemical mixture added in. You don't ever want to grill meat with it. The stench is enough to make you a vegetarian," Dan said. For the first time, they both broke a smile.

"You got that right," Gloria said. "But—why? We suspected Rush and Stu, but why'd they do it and what's your sister got to do with this?"

"It's kind of a long story," Dan said.

"And we have a long ambulance ride," Gloria said. "So tell me."

"Well, my sister Jenny and I grew up on a farm near Westport. Our parents were killed in a car accident when we were little, and our grandparents raised us. I was older, and I always felt responsible for her—I tried to look out for her."

"I went to high school with Rush and Stu. They were the rich kids, and we were from the other side of the tracks. Everybody knew they were into drugs. After high school, they both went off to college. I heard they got kicked out of at least two schools before they came back home to Westport."

"They started throwing these wild parties, and Jenny got invited to one. Jenny thought it would be cool to party with the rich kids. But she did more than party—she got hooked on drugs, too, and after a while she owed them money. A lot of money. Before you and Ashante moved in, Rush and Stu rented that house where you live now. While they lived there, my sister would crash with them on a regular basis. They had her so strung out, she would do anything to get high."

Dan paused and looked up at the ceiling of the ambulance, his face as still as stone. Gloria wasn't sure if he was in pain, or if he was just collecting his thoughts. "Dan, you okay?" she said.

"It's just that this is going to kill my grandparents," he said. "They're very religious, and they always taught us to treat everyone fairly. I've never been in trouble with the law. This whole thing is tearing my insides out."

Gloria could see he was truly remorseful. She reached out and squeezed his hand.

"Dan," she said gently, "how does this connect to the cross burning? I still don't understand."

"Rush and Stu pushed drugs not only to the frats on campus, but to any student and townie looking to score. Jenny said they kept large amounts of dope hidden in the attic."

Gloria felt like every nerve ending in her body was suddenly on high alert. *The muddy footprints in the hallway—right outside the attic door!* It was all beginning to make sense.

"Dan," she said, "if Dr. Oliver's plan works, we'll be able to set a trap. Well, the police will anyway. Officer Rodriquez is meeting us at the hospital. Will you talk to him and tell him all of this? Dr. Oliver thinks Thomas and Carlson will be sent to pick up Rush and Stu. If you're willing to help us, I think we can finally get justice."

Dan gave her a sincere look. "I'll do whatever it takes!" he said.

"Good. Now you should probably get some rest. Officer Rodriquez will fill us in on the rest of the plan when we get to the hospital. Oh, and Dan, one last thing. I forgive you."

"God bless you," Dan sighed. He turned away so Gloria wouldn't see the tears in his eyes.

## CHAPTER TWENTY FIVE

The bus ride back to Lakeside was filled with worried speculation over the morning's events. Rumors were flying fast and furious. The group was so unnerved by what had happened, that no one noticed Stu and Rush hadn't joined them on the bus.

With most of the conversation focused on Dan's welfare, the faculty carefully addressed the students' concerns while trying to keep everyone's emotions in check. To divert their attention, they finally succeeded in getting the students to share what they'd learned from the retreat.

"I never had a problem with people of other races, but I never had a close relationship with any of them either," Chris said. "I always thought the best approach was to stay out of their way. This retreat showed me what I've been missing by passing up on friendships because of the color of someone's skin. I made some really good friends at the retreat—Chuck and Kwame, to name a couple. They wiped the basketball court with me, but they also made me feel accepted. I wouldn't have missed that experience for the world."

Judith explained how the retreat had opened her eyes to seeing that diversity benefits everyone. She announced that she would ensure that her sorority chapter would actively seek out African American pledges.

Lori announced that the *Campus Tempo* would be adding a special section highlighting other cultures and addressing the concerns of students of color on campus. "I am also going to propose changes so the campus newspaper can't be censored so easily," she said. "In light of this scandal, I think the newspaper will have a larger role to play in exposing the truth."

Chuck and Donna shared details about their new interracial social club. "I've learned that we all have misconceptions that we have to overcome, in order to get to what's real," Donna said, looking in Chuck's direction.

"I learned it's not bad spending half, or even all, of your free time with someone of a different race!" Chuck said, bringing laughter from everyone.

Even Ashante shared a few words. "Although I've seen the worst in people, this retreat has also shown me some of the best," she said. "The best part for me is, I don't feel like a victim anymore."

Jamal left his seat with Kwame and walked to the back of the bus. He slid into the seat next to Mark Serra.

"I owe you an apology," Jamal said.

"For what?" Mark asked, a surprised look on his face.

"You were right. We do have a lot in common. People judge me by my skin color. They judge you by your sexual orientation. I know I did, and that's not right."

"I'm used to it," Mark said. "Thanks for the apology, though— that part I'm not used to."

"It was necessary for me," Jamal said. "I get so caught up in my own problems and causes, that I treat people pretty badly sometimes. I misjudged Bruce. I almost overlooked Gloria completely. And I never really gave you a chance. Hopefully, I won't make those same mistakes in the future."

"Hey, man, that means a lot," Mark said. He put his arm around Jamal's shoulders, and Jamal returned the half-embrace. Several students snickered, but Jamal laughed it off. He understood for the first time that anger didn't need to be his first response.

Donna and Chuck snuggled contentedly in their seats. Other couples did the same. Ashante and Bruce spent the time planning strategy for Bruce's assembly the following day. Chris and Kwame argued good-naturedly over who was the greatest running back of all time.

***

Ten miles from Lakeside, Stu and Rush sat in the back of a Westport squad car.

"Man," Stu said, "are we glad you guys picked us up instead of the campus cops—or worse yet, the local authorities."

"Don't thank us," Sgt. Carlson said angrily. "We didn't exactly do it out of deep affection. You idiots are damn lucky that Severson called us."

"So what's the status," Rush said. "Did you get the shit out of the house this weekend, or what?"

"Hell, no," Officer Thomas said. "That damn Rodriquez has been driving past the house every ten minutes."

Sgt. Carlson glared at Stu and Rush in the rearview mirror. "Yeah, and that nosy reporter, Walsh, was asking questions at the station. We had to watch our backs. And what did you losers do? You panicked and tried to waste Dan. What were you thinking?"

"Hey man, he was going to rat us out," Rush said. "We had to do something!"

"You should have called us," Carlson said. "We would have done it right. Now we're stuck tying up the loose ends because you two ass wipes can't be trusted. You've screwed this up from the beginning, and I'm sure we can't trust you to keep your mouths shut now. We gotta figure out how to cut our losses."

"Hey man, we can work this out, there's no need to—."

Stu's cell phone rang. Quickly, he flipped it open. "Who is this?" he said.

"It's Dan. Listen carefully."

"What the hell you doing calling me, punk?" Stu said. He covered the receiver with his hand. "It's that damn snitch," he said.

"Listen, fool," Dan said. I'm trying to save your asses. I'm at the hospital. I just talked to Rodriguez—the bus hasn't gotten back yet. You bozos have two hours to get the shit. You have to make sure that Ashante doesn't go to the house. Have Severson meet the bus. Do whatever it takes. Gloria is here with me. I sent her down the lobby to get me something to read. This is your last chance. Just get in, get the coke, and get the hell out of there."

"He says we can get the shit," Stu told the others. "Nobody's in the house."

"What about Rodriquez?" he asked Dan.

"He's standing outside my door. I can see him through the glass. He's here to question me. He was the only one patrolling the house. Gloria said he was doing it as a personal favor while they were away at the retreat."

"What will you tell him, snitch?"

"I won't tell him squat, but you gotta make Jenny's debt go away."

"If we get the stuff, then the slate will be clean," Stu promised.

"All of the debt, man, I'm not bullshitting. We never want anything to do with you again, you understand?"

"Yeah, yeah," Stu said, "but what about that little rope incident?"

"I won't press charges. Your daddy's lawyers can arrange it. I just want this whole mess to be over. Oh, wait—someone's coming. I gotta go."

Stu hung up the phone and explained the situation to Thomas and Carlson.

"If I can reach Severson and he agrees to stall Ashante, it looks like we may get out of this hole," Stu said. "You'll get your dope and we won't go to jail. We don't have much time, so step on it."

As Carlson hit the gas, Stu and Rush exchanged a very satisfied smile.

***

Officer Rodriguez patted Dan on the shoulder. "Good job," he said.

Dan turned to Steve Walsh, who was sitting on the edge of the bed, taking notes. "Did you get that?" Dan asked.

"Every word," Walsh said. "Looks like this is going to be my lucky day."

"Let's hope they fell for it," said Gloria, who was perched on the chair opposite the bed.

"Trust me," Dan said, "they only have one thing on their minds right now."

***

As the bus approached the Student Union, Professor Reese looked at Mr. Brown, one of the faculty chaperones, and smiled, looking tired but relieved.

"Quite a different atmosphere in here, isn't it?" Reese said.

"I'll say. It wasn't a waste of time, was it?" Brown said. "Although, the true test still lies ahead. It will be interesting to see if this holds."

"That's true," Reese said. "But no matter what, thanks to Dr. Oliver, I have a feeling Lakeside will never be the same again."

Dean Severson was waiting at the curb when the bus pulled to a stop. He rapped impatiently on the door and hurried aboard as soon as the driver let him in. The students stopped talking as soon as they saw him.

"I've been informed by your chaperones about the unfortunate incident involving Dan Trent," Severson said. "We may need

181

statements from you, so please remain on the bus until your name is called. This shouldn't take more than an hour or so."

A grumbling of protest broke out.

"Are you kidding me?"

"No way!"

"I didn't see anything—why would the cops want to talk to me!"

Ms. Ford calmed the complaints by suggesting they wait in the Union. "That way they can at least stretch their legs and use the bathrooms," she said.

Severson reluctantly agreed, but not before telling them that they all must stay together. For two hours, they waited in a small meeting room on the Union's second floor.

"I thought they wanted to question us or something," Chris griped.

Kwame laughed. "Leave it to a white dude to be upset that the cops don't want to talk to him!"

Finally, Severson stepped into the room. "You're all free to go," he told them.

Instead of heading home, Ashante and Jamal rushed to the recording studio. After cleaning up the tape, Ashante couldn't contain her excitement. She tore off her headset and pushed it into Jamal's hands.

"Here, wait until you hear this!" she exclaimed. "We've got those pricks now! They were in our house!"

"Let's hear it," Jamal said.

With the background noise filtered out, the recorded sounds were much easier to hear. Ashante's voice was clear as she answered the phone and had the brief exchange with the caller. A long period of silence followed, coinciding with Ashante leaving the house to find the burning cross. Then there was a loud thud, followed by whispering male voices.

"Why don't you watch where you're going?" a voice whispered hoarsely.

"I would if you'd stop shoving me, Rush," a second voice whined.

"We gotta hurry! Let's grab the shit and get the hell out of here. What are you doing? Get away from the window before someone sees you!"

"Man, that sucker's really burning now!"

"You can gloat later, Stu! Get your ass over here and help me move this."

"Move what?"

"Those stupid bitches put furniture in front of the attic door."

There was a sliding sound, like furniture being moved.

"Damn, they're coming in the house! Let's get outta here!"

"What about the coke?"

"No time. We'll have to try again later."

"But if we don't get the dope, Thomas and Carlson are going to waste our asses!"

"Yeah, well, if we get caught, it's all over. Move!"

They heard the sound of retreating footsteps and a door slamming.

"I can't believe this was all over drugs!" said Jamal. "I can't believe they would go that far."

"I can't believe I got it all on tape!" Ashante said, hopping around. "We even got their names! And those cops' names, too!"

As the tape continued to run, more footsteps were heard and a voice Ashante identified as Sgt. Thomas spoke. "Good, footprints!" he said. "Those losers have been here. We can split now."

"So he didn't use the bathroom that night after all," Ashante said. "That bastard!"

"We're going to shake this campus to its foundation," Jamal said, "but over dope. You know the media will jump at the chance to focus on that, rather than racism."

"At least we're going to nail those assholes," Ashante said. "They won't be able to do it again."

# CHAPTER TWENTY SIX

At Monday's assembly, the auditorium filled to overflowing. The crowd was drawn by the shocking revelations they had read in *The Herald* that morning and heard discussed all over campus. Monday's banner headline read, "WESTPORT COPS BUSTED IN DRUG SCANDAL," with a photo of Thomas and Carlson in handcuffs, being led away by Officer Rodriguez.

A beaming Steve Walsh was on hand at the front of the auditorium, accepting kudos for his scoop. Walsh's sidebar column on the corrupt cops explained how they came to control the local drug trade:

*"...Corrupt officers George Thomas and Ralph Carlson appear to have gotten their start through a routine traffic stop. Two years ago, they caught Lakeside University students Rush Haughman and Stu Barton in a speed trap. During an illegal car search, Thomas and Carlson discovered a stash of drugs. They compelled the students to identify their supplier and become their partners by threatening them with jail time."*

*"Their lucrative scheme worked well until the students were evicted from their drug house, leaving a stash of cocaine behind, worth more than $500,000...Yesterday, they were found in the house's attic, trying to retrieve the drugs. They were arrested by a team from Campus Police, led by LU Officer Carlos Rodriquez..."*

Bruce called the assembly to order. With him on the dais were Gloria, Ashante, Jamal, Dan Trent, Dr. Oliver, Dean Severson and President Horning.

"You've all seen *The Herald*, so you know about the drugs and the corrupt police officers," Bruce began. "Rush and Stu have been charged with attempted murder of Dan Trent, burglary, and a variety of drug offenses. Steve Walsh's article confirmed that officers Thomas and Carlson were Rush and Stu's drug dealing partners. They are being charged with burglary for breaking into the house to recover the drugs, and with possession with intent to deliver."

"Ashante had a tape that proved Rush and Stu were responsible for the cross burning, and that those two cops were involved in the cover-up. That tape has been handed over to the authorities, so you can expect that additional charges will be filed. I know a lot of this sounds incredible, but it really did happen. Dan has asked to say a few words to help us understand why."

Dan stepped up to the microphone. An expectant hush fell over the room.

"I want to apologize to everyone," he said softly, staring blankly ahead. "I knew all along who was behind the cross burning. Although I called Gloria the night it happened, I was too afraid to tell her who did it. I'm not trying to excuse what I did, just explain it." He turned to face Gloria with a deeply distraught look on his face.

"The night Rush and Stu burned the cross," Dan continued, "there was a third person with them. This person didn't have anything to do with the cross burning. She just drove those two cowards to Gloria and Ashante's house. She owed Rush and Stu money for drugs, and they forced her to be their driver. She had no idea what they were going to do."

"That person is my sister Jenny. My grandparents and I checked her into rehab last week so she can get clean. She's holding her own, but it will always be day to day."

"I was afraid if I spoke up about who was responsible, they would try to blame everything on her. They also made Jenny put a death threat in Jamal's mail box and make some threatening phone calls, which she deeply regrets." He was silent for a moment, waiting for the crowd's reaction.

"I played another role in this," Dan added quietly. "I stole Ashante's tape from her purse. I did it because I was afraid there might be something on it that would incriminate my sister. Actually, Rush ordered Jenny to steal it, but I convinced her to let me take care of it, because I didn't want her to get into any more trouble. But we never would have known the tape existed if Dean Severson hadn't told Rush and Stu about it. He told them they had to get the tape and destroy it."

Todd Severson leapt up from his chair, howling in protest as he grabbed the microphone. "That's outrageous!" Severson thundered. "You have no right to level that accusation! That's grounds for expulsion, do you understand?"

But the crowd was already on its feet, shouting and hollering over Severson's words. Finally, Dr. Oliver stepped forward and called for silence.

"Dean Severson," he said, "are you denying this young man's charge?"

"Damn right, I am!"

"You had nothing to do with helping to cover up Stu and Rush's involvement?"

"Cover up? No, of course not! On this school's honor, I've done nothing but try to get to the bottom of this."

"'On this school's honor'," Dr. Oliver repeated. "Interesting word choice. In that case, I have a recording I think your students deserve to hear."

Dr. Oliver pulled a tape recorder from his pocket. He held it up to the microphone and hit *play*. The audience listened to the recorded phone call in stunned silence. There was Severson, admitting to everything.

The crowd was enraged. "Arrest them! Arrest them!" they began to yell.

Horning pushed Dr. Oliver out of the way and stepped up to the microphone. "Just calm down, everyone," he tried to say, but the chanting only grew louder.

"Jail them both! Jail them both!"

As the students continued chanting, Horning and Severson exchanged a nervous glance. They grabbed their coats and hurried off the stage. As they approached the side door, Officer Rodriguez emerged from the darkness.

"Going somewhere, gentlemen?" he asked.

The students' cries filled the auditorium as Officer Rodriquez escorted Horning and Severson outside.

Bruce stepped up to the podium and tried to quiet the crowd. "Why don't we let Dan finish his story," he said.

Dan cleared his throat as the audience settled down. "Rush and Stu used to live in the house before Gloria and Ashante rented it," he continued. "When they got evicted, their landlord brought the sheriff with him. Rather than risk getting busted, they ended up leaving their stash hidden in the attic."

"They tried to break into the house a couple of times, but someone was always at home. When Sgt. Thomas found out they had left the stash, he gave them 24 hours to return the drugs or the cash, or else."

"But why did they burn that cross?" someone yelled out.

"They needed a strong enough diversion to let them sneak into the house undetected. Jenny said they also thought it would be fun to scare the new black girls. I don't think they expected things would get this far out of control."

When there was a pause in the questions, Bruce stepped up to the microphone. "Before we left on the retreat, this campus was almost at a standstill," he said. "A lot of that was because most of the student organizations supported the administration's investigation, and we agreed to cease demonstrating until that investigation was complete. This caused BSO, and probably rightfully so, to think that all of the other student organizations had turned their backs on them."

"Just as Jamal suspected, there never was an administrative investigation. In fact, both Dean Severson and President Horning were involved in the cover-up of the cross burning. I've been informed that a criminal investigation will be launched into their involvement in this incident and others in the past, involving Rush and Stu."

When the ensuing uproar died down, Gloria stepped to the microphone.

"Although drugs were behind the cross burning, we now know that racism was Rush and Stu's true drug of choice, and the reason things got out of hand. Drugs are used to cloud one's perception of reality, just as racism is used to cloud the reality of one's perception of others. I know racism hasn't ended because this case is solved, but I do have reason to be optimistic, and it's mainly because of you."

"This past weekend, we took a giant step forward in starting to listen to each other. I'm really grateful we went on this retreat. It's surprising how much we were able to accomplish, once we started communicating. Let's pledge to keep talking," she said, as the audience cheered. "I want Jamal to say a few words before we close, because I couldn't have made it through this without him."

After briefly embracing Gloria, Jamal faced the audience with a smile. "At first, I didn't believe a retreat was a solution for our problems, because I thought it would distract us from the real issues at hand," Jamal said. "I was wrong. Sometimes we get so caught up in the cause that we can't see what's really happening."

"The retreat was the catalyst that allowed us to solve this crisis. We were forced to talk to and listen to each other, whether we wanted to or not. I learned a lot this weekend, and I think I discovered what true leadership is all about. What you heard from Dan and Bruce were pieces of a puzzle that have all come together.

The mastermind who is responsible for helping us solve this puzzle is Dr. Wendell Oliver."

The auditorium exploded in applause.

"Dr. Oliver showed us the importance of what Gloria just said—true communication, whether it was in a peace tent or just spending time together," Jamal said, as a few chuckles rippled through the auditorium. "I also discovered something else this weekend. Actually, it was something that I was missing—a special person."

"She was there all along, and I was too blind to see her. She and her roommate Ashante are two of the bravest people I know. Would you help me show some love to Ashante and my special lady, Gloria?" The audience stood as one and applauded, as Gloria embraced Jamal, the tears flowing down her cheeks.

Dr. Oliver stepped up to the podium, and the crowd quieted.

"I want to thank Gloria, too," he said, "because she helped me to rekindle my passion for this kind of work. I think she and Ashante now realize they gain strength and confidence every time they face their fears."

"I know this has been a difficult time for your university, but yet there is hope. Those of you who attended the retreat have learned you're better when you work together. That's the key. You've begun to trust one another, and that will open the door to understanding. The events you have witnessed over the past few weeks could have easily made you become disillusioned and bitter. It is much more difficult to maintain optimism in the face of such adversity, but that is exactly what is needed now."

"Rush, Stu, and those Westport police officers have all shown you the worst in human behavior. It's up to you to model the best behavior, and to make this campus a place where everyone feels valued and welcome at the table. Jamal, Malcolm used to say, 'you can preach a greater sermon with your life than with your lips.'"

Dr. Oliver invited Bruce, Gloria, Ashante and Jamal to join hands and raise them skyward, as he led the assembly in a triumphant chant, accompanied by cheers and tears from the students.

"Unity, through diversity!"

The assembly ended on that high note. As the last few students were leaving, Gloria stayed back to thank Dr. Oliver one final time.

"Many people question why I do this type of work," he told her. "Sometimes when things are rough, I wonder, myself. But on days like today, my reason is crystal clear. We really accomplished something here, something worthwhile. I think Lakeside will see its way through this."

"The wounds will heal, but what about the scars?" Gloria asked.

"They will serve as reminders," Dr. Oliver answered gently. "Only through remembering can we avoid repeating the mistakes of the past."

## ABOUT THE AUTHOR

Dr. Charles "Chuck" Taylor is a professor in the school of education at a small private Midwestern college. Although he has written and edited over 10 books, this is his first novel. The idea for the novel came after Chuck had conducted several student retreats around the country.

Dr. Taylor says the students he's worked with left a profound impression. *"A group of caring but skeptical students assemble themselves to dialogue over some of the most sensitive issues their campus faces. At first they are really hesitant about what they say, being careful not to offend, but the structured activities slowly force them to be honest, rather than tactful. When their honesty is not viewed in a judgmental way then genuine communication is possible. It is during those moments of "authentic" conversation that true feelings emerge."*

Dr. Taylor says this novel is really a tribute to those students who dare to take risks cross culturally.

In addition to writing a novel, Chuck has written a full-length children's musical, a highly acclaimed documentary on the Milwaukee Civil Rights movement and continues to serve as a national consultant in the area of diversity and inclusion.